"It wasn't your fa[ult]"

"Whoever did this is scum," Sundance insisted. "Help me catch him before he hurts someone else."

"I don't remember," Iris whispered, shaking her head in a pathetic, scared little rabbit motion that tore at his heart. "I don't think I want to remember. What if he's someone I know? What if he's watching me all the time, waiting to do it again?"

"That's not going to happen," he said, fighting to keep the growl from his voice. "We're going to catch him."

"You don't know that."

"I know that I won't stop until I do."

Seeing her so broken, so torn apart mentally, awakened a grizzly bear of rage that made him want to go on a rampage. But he couldn't do that, not when he needed to keep a calm head in order to catch whoever did this.

"He's out there. Every time I close my eyes he's there, watching me. Waiting."

"I'm here." No one was going to touch her. He'd make sure of it. He felt pressure against his bicep as she tentatively laid her head against him. "No one is going to touch you."

★ ★ ★

Dear Reader,

Some stories are difficult to write, but the characters burst from your imagination and demand every resource you've got because their story is so important. This is what happened with Iris and Sundance. Set on an Indian reservation in Washington State, this story called to my natural Native American heritage. The research was daunting at times, but the end result was wholly gratifying. I hope Iris's courage and Sundance's strength buoy you during their tumultuous and, at times, dark journey toward love.

This is the first in my Native Country series. Next up, Mya Jonson and Angelo Tucker, another couple who had an important story to tell and one likely to tug at your heart.

Hearing from readers is a special joy. Please feel free to drop me a line via email through my website at www.kimberlyvanmeter.com or through snail mail at Kimberly Van Meter, P.O. BOX 2210, Oakdale, CA 95361.

Kimberly Van Meter

KIMBERLY VAN METER

Sworn to Protect

ROMANTIC SUSPENSE

Recycling programs
for this product may
not exist in your area.

ISBN-13: 978-0-373-27736-0

SWORN TO PROTECT

Printed in U.S.A.

Books by Kimberly Van Meter

Romantic Suspense

To Catch a Killer #1622
Guarding the Socialite #1638
★★*A Chance in the Night* #1700
★★*Secrets in a Small Town* #1706

Harlequin Romantic Suspense

†*Sworn to Protect* #1666

Superromance

The Truth About Family #1391
★*Father Material* #1433
★*Return to Emmett's Mill* #1469
A Kiss to Remember #1485
★*An Imperfect Match* #1513
★*Kids on the Doorstep* #1577
★*A Man Worth Loving* #1600
★*Trusting the Bodyguard* #1627
★★*The Past Between Us* #1694

†Native Country
★Home in Emmett's Mill
★★Mama Jo's Boys

KIMBERLY VAN METER

wrote her first book at sixteen and finally achieved publication in December 2006. She writes for Harlequin Superromance and Harlequin Romantic Suspense.

She and her husband of seventeen years have three children, three cats and always a houseful of friends, family and fun.

There's a special pride felt by those who share Native blood. This is dedicated to the scores of people who honor their Native American ancestry by refusing to forget who they are and where they come from.

To my great grandmother Ella "Tootsie" Rhoan for trying to teach me our Native language when I was young and for coming to my fourth grade class to show us how to make acorn meal. I was too young to appreciate what a gift you were giving.

Chapter 1

A parade of pain marched across Iris Beaudoin's body as she slowly opened her eyes and squinted against the harsh white light. Her best friend, Dr. Mya Jonson, was staring down at her, an expression of fear and worry warring with her need to fix what had been broken.

"Wh-ere am I?" she managed to croak. Her clothes were gone and she was wearing a hospital gown, which meant she was at the urgent care facility, Healthy Living, where she worked with Mya. "M-Mya? What happened?"

"I don't know, honey, but you were found alongside the road before the Pititchu Bridge. You've been beaten pretty bad," Mya answered, gingerly clutching Iris's hand. "Do you remember anything?"

Iris swallowed and closed her eyes against the pain radiating from every pore of her body. "Hurts," she whispered. "I can't think…"

"Okay, honey, don't worry. We're going to get you fixed up and then we're going to find out who did this to you."

Iris nodded in a faint movement but even that small action cost her. Mya rubbed her hand and gave it a light squeeze, then said, "I have to do an SAE," she said, her voice breaking.

SAE…Iris was a nurse and she knew what that meant. Sexual Assault Exam. A tear leaked down her cheek and she nodded again. "Okay," she whispered.

"I'm so sorry, but we have to know," Mya said. "I'll make it quick. I promise."

Iris squeezed her eyes shut and allowed her knees to part even as she fought the shuddering cries that felt trapped in her chest. Someone had assaulted her, that much was apparent, but her brain was fuzzy in the details.

She remembered…being at the bar…dancing… karaoke…and then nothing.

Iris winced as Mya swabbed her insides, quickly, efficiently, yet still Iris wanted to scream at the violation.

Finished, Mya packaged the wet mount for DNA testing and then made quick work of the pelvic exam. Iris was thankful for her friend's sensitivity but she was nearing hysteria. The blank spots in her memory were frightening her as much as the realization that someone had done this to her.

"We had to take your clothes for evidence," Mya said in apology. "But I don't think you're going to want them back anyway, honey, because they're pretty messed up."

"S'ok," she mumbled, knowing her clothes were the least of her problems at the moment. She watched her best friend fight for composure and waited for Mya to tell her. But she was stalling, bringing a blanket to lay it over her, fussing over her comfort when nothing would've made a difference.

She met her friend's brokenhearted eyes. "The SAE…it showed I was raped." It was a statement, not a question, and the realization sank into her slowly awakening consciousness like a brick to the bottom of a lake. She'd been raped.

Mya drew a halting breath as she jerked a nod. "There were serious abrasions…consistent with forcible…" She swallowed and a tear escaped Mya's control. She wiped it away quickly but another followed. "Oh, Iris…"

Iris lifted her chin but it trembled. What was there to say? Both turned at the discreet knock at the door. Sundance Jonson, Mya's brother and the tribal police officer, walked in, presumably to take her statement. She turned her head, groaning. Not Sundance. She couldn't let him see her this way. "Not you," she said, wanting to curl on her side but the pain prevented it. "Someone else."

"Iris, Sundance is the only officer on the rez, you know that. He's here to help."

"Not him," she whispered, covering her face with her hands. "Go away."

"Iris…" Mya tried again, her tone distressed, but Iris didn't want to hear it. She wanted to get off that bed and run, and if she couldn't run, she wanted to crawl. Iris felt herself folding in, anything to avoid telling Sundance what had happened to her, or rather, what she didn't know had happened.

Iris and Sundance had history—not romantic—but rather childhood history. Iris and Mya were best friends their entire lives, and so she'd known Sundance, as well.

But they'd never been friends. And he'd never seen her as anything more than his little sister's troublesome sidekick. That would've been fine, if she hadn't awoken one morning with a completely different feeling about Sundance than she'd had before. Suddenly, she saw the man, not the overbearing, control freak that she'd always seen before.

She'd gone to the bar in an attempt to get Sundance off her mind. She didn't want to see Sundance as anything other than the annoying big brother of her best friend who lived to antagonize her. The fact that she'd begun to see him as a *man* had disconcerted her to the point of irrationality.

A sob remained trapped in her throat. How had this happened? Her whole life had been tipped on end and it felt as though everything she held dear had fallen to shatter on the floor. How could she bear to look at herself in the mirror ever again? How could anyone else see anything aside from what had happened to her?

"Iris…" The softness of his voice nearly undid her completely. "Tell me who did this so I can bring them to justice," he urged.

"I don't know who did this," she answered, wiping at the tear slipping down her cheek. "I don't remember."

"Did you check for drugs?" he murmured to Mya.

"Yes, we'll do a tox screen with the blood and urine samples but they won't be ready right away," Mya answered. "We'll screen for every known date rape drug. Ketamine, GHB, Rohypnol…if there's anything in her system we'll find it."

Iris closed her eyes, wishing she could block out their voices as they discussed her case. She knew both Mya and Sundance were doing their jobs but she couldn't handle the routine just yet. "Please go away," she whispered, meaning both of them. She turned to meet Mya's questioning gaze. "I just want to be alone for a minute."

Mya nodded but the worry remained stationed in her eyes. "Okay, honey. Just a few minutes, though. I need to scrape underneath your fingernails still."

"Right," Iris managed, but her vision blurred as more tears followed. Then Mya hustled Sundance from the room to give her the privacy she'd asked for.

Her body ached and throbbed while her numbed brain wrestled with one question: Why?

Sundance struggled to remain impartial, to stay cool but inside a white-hot poker of rage punctured his good intentions. "Is she going to be all right?" he asked, his jaw grinding on the words.

"I think so," Mya answered, wrapping her arms around herself. "What kind of monster does this?" she demanded in a harsh whisper so that her voice didn't carry to Iris in the trauma room. "There's not a piece of skin that doesn't carry some kind of mark. It's a miracle she's alive, and honestly, I think that's what this devil had in mind. When I think of how close she came to…" Mya shuddered. "I just get sick to my stomach."

Sundance understood his sister's anguish. Seeing Iris—a woman he'd known his entire life and had most often found irritating, infuriating and intrusive—all tore up caused something inside him to roar like a wounded bear, swiping and snarling at anyone with the misfortune to get too close. And the reaction shocked him.

"I'm going to have to question her," he said, still processing his own reaction to the situation, trying to put it into perspective. Of course, he was bothered. It was his job to safeguard the tribe, to be the one to protect the people. To think there was someone on the reservation who could do this to one of their own… Sundance didn't want to believe it. An outsider had to have done this. And he was going to find whoever it was and show him a little justice—American-Indian style.

Mya hesitated, something plainly causing her to temper her tongue, and he furrowed his brow at her expression. "What's wrong?"

"It's just that you and Iris…you haven't always had the best track record with each other. I don't know that she'll open up to you. Maybe I could ask the questions for you."

"No, I have to ask them. I'm sorry but that's procedure." He understood Mya's motivation and he didn't fault her for it. His sister had a loving and protective heart, just one of the many reasons he thought the world of her. But he had a job to do. He met Mya's eyes and gave her the most heartfelt assurance he could offer as he promised to be gentle. "I know we've had our differences, but I won't let that get in the way of doing anything and everything I can to find whoever did this. I promise."

Mya searched his gaze and found truth. She exhaled and nodded. "I know you'll do your best for Iris. I trust in you, my brother."

Sundance gave his sister a reassuring squeeze on her shoulder and then returned to the room where Iris remained curled in as close to a fetal position as her injuries would allow.

Again that swell of rage welled inside him and he had to force it down. "Iris…"

"Sundance, please, *just go away,*" she pleaded with him, eliciting a wince on his part for Iris had never, in her life, pleaded with anyone. She barreled, she cajoled, she went so far as to manipulate but she *never* begged. But she was doing it now, with him, and it nearly broke the grip he had on the gates holding everything in check.

"You know I can't do that. I can't catch who did this unless you help me."

When she realized he wasn't going anywhere she played with the swollen tissue on her bottom lip and stared at the floor. When she finally answered, it was without any emotion. "I don't know anything. I told you, I can't remember."

"Okay, let's start from what you do remember," he suggested softly, but she only squeezed her eyes shut and sealed her lips. "C'mon, let's start from the beginning of the night. You remember that, right?"

"Yes," she answered, an edge returning to her voice. "But what does that matter? Remembering what I wore and what song I sang for karaoke isn't going to tell me who managed to drag me from a bar full of people to some secluded place where the guy raped and beat me. So just go away, Sundance. I don't…want to talk about this anymore."

That last part came out as a choked whisper and his hands tightened around his pen as she plainly locked him out for reasons he couldn't really fathom.

"Forget our troubles from the past, Iris. All I want to do is help you. We can do this together." He tried again, coming at her from a different angle, but she wouldn't have any of it. Her silence was answer enough.

He swallowed a frustrated breath, not wanting to push, but needing to anyway. He felt rather than saw Mya hovering at the doorway and turned to find her standing there. "I'll come back tomorrow, Iris," he told her, giving her fair warning. As he passed Mya in the doorway, he murmured, "Try talking some sense into her, please. Maybe she'll listen to you."

Mya nodded but her expression was bleak. "I'll do what I can…she's so hurt, Sonny. I've never seen her so—"

"I know," he acknowledged grimly. "Me neither."

Iris may not want his help but she was going to get it anyway.

Someone was going down for what they'd done.

That was a promise.

Chapter 2

Sundance strode into the Healthy Living urgent care facility and went straight to the reception desk. Betty Whitefeather, the ancient front desk receptionist, waved him through and he entered the side door, heading for Mya's private office. He was in luck, she was sitting there, scribbling some patient notes. When she saw him standing in the doorway, she closed the file and looked at him expectantly. "What's up?" she asked.

"Has she been in?" he asked, cutting straight to the point. Mya's fallen expression was all the answer he needed. "She can't hide in her house for the rest of her life. Someone needs to get her to start living again."

Mya shifted into protective mode. "It's only been a few weeks. Cut her some slack. Have any leads surfaced on the case?"

"No," he admitted grimly, chewing his lip. And he'd given more resources to Iris's assault than any other case currently on his desk. "Forensics are a slow process. But something is bound to turn up."

"I hope so," Mya murmured, but Sundance could tell she was doubtful they'd ever catch the man who'd brutalized Iris. Although she was defensive of her best friend, she said, "I am worried about her. She's…" Mya hesitated, caught between sharing too much and helping her friend. "She's not dealing well with everything. I can't get her to leave the house at all."

There was something Mya wasn't saying. Sundance could tell by the way she refused to meet his stare that there was more. Sundance knew he had to see Iris, even if under the guise of investigative work.

"I'm going out there," he announced, knowing Mya's reaction would be negative. He wasn't disappointed. When his sister started to shake her head, saying it wasn't a good idea, he shut her down firmly. "I need to see if she remembers anything now that some time has passed since the initial shock, and she's not picking up her phone."

"She doesn't want visitors," Mya said. "She's not up to it yet. And I don't think you badgering her about the case is going to help matters. She needs to do this in her own time."

His tone gentled. "I'm not going to push her too hard. But if too much time passes, we might lose the opportunity to dredge up what she can remember. I want to catch this guy before he does it to someone else. Iris is a fighter. She's going to get through this," he promised with true conviction. He'd never known a more stubborn woman than Iris Beaudoin and he couldn't imagine her allowing anything to take her down for long.

Although Mya nodded, worry still shone in her eyes. "She's not the same, Sonny. I don't know what to do," she admitted. She wiped at the tears gathering at the corners of her eyes. Sundance hated to see his sister cry. He gave her shoulder a reassuring squeeze and she seemed to take comfort in the knowledge that he was there for her. She straightened and nodded, ready to put her faith in him to fix things. "Maybe you can do what I can't seem to manage. But remember, she's so fragile right now. Go easy on her."

Sundance nodded but he made no promises. He'd have to see for himself what was happening with Iris before he knew how to handle the situation.

All he knew at this point was that Iris hadn't left her home in the three weeks since she left the hospital. Mya brought her supplies, but otherwise she accepted no visitors. For all intents and purposes, she'd locked herself away in her house.

And that definitely wasn't the Iris Beaudoin he'd known since she and Mya were in kindergarten together and he was in the third grade.

The Iris he knew was fearless, prideful, stubborn, a royal pain in his ass, in-your-face woman who laughed at challenges and never failed to gleefully insert herself into other people's business without apology.

He couldn't let that Iris wither and crumple in on herself, and if it took him to rile her up and draw her out, he'd do it. Whether she liked it or not.

Iris heard the sharp rap at her front door and ignored it just as she had whenever someone happened to stop by. She knew Mya was still at the urgent care center but even so, Mya wouldn't knock because she had a key and would just walk in. So whoever was knocking—insistently and loudly—would eventually go away when they realized Iris wasn't going to receive them.

The darkened interior of her usually sunny bedroom was her sanctuary and her prison. She'd stripped the gauzy panels of her bedroom windows, replacing them with dark, heavy blankets that blocked any hint of sunshine as well as prevented prying eyes from seeing in. Each time she felt the stirrings of strength to face the outside, she shrank away with fear that he was out there, watching her, laughing. When she slept she fought phantom hands that grabbed and violated. She often woke screaming, soaking in her own panic-driven sweat, stinking of terror and helplessness. So she caught catnaps when her body could no longer fight the exhaustion, but she stopped sleeping through the night to avoid the nightmares. Mya had offered to write her a prescription for something to help her sleep but Iris had balked at the idea. The thought of being unable to rouse herself from her dreams was too much like that night, being unable to help herself as a stranger had raped and beaten her. She shuddered violently and she burrowed deeper into the blankets heaped on her bed. In spite of the summer heat, she couldn't seem to warm her body. It was as if her internal temperature had been permanently set to deep freeze.

At least the knocking had stopped.

Then she heard the front door opening and she scrambled out of the bed, grabbing the baseball bat she kept by her bedside now. She'd thought of getting a gun but that would require leaving her house and facing people.

It was probably Mya, the logical side of her brain offered, but the logic was drowned out by the panicked part of her that was in complete control right now. Her grip tightened on the neck of the worn wood.

"Iris?" a voice called out, and recognition caused her to stiffen in alarm.

"Sundance?" she answered, her voice scratchy from disuse. "Is that you?" He followed her voice and rounded the corner to the threshold of her bedroom where she still stood in the shadows with a raised baseball bat. He peered into the darkness and then flipped the light switch. She stumbled from the sudden wash of bright light and dropped the bat to crawl to the safety of her bed. "Go away," she demanded, pulling the covers over her head. "I don't want any visitors." *Least of all you*.

But he didn't go away. Instead he walked to the window and she heard him taking down her blankets, flooding the room with natural light. She felt the sunshine filling the room and she burrowed deeper into her bedding. She didn't want sunshine. She wanted darkness and solitude.

"I need to talk to you," Sundance said, ignoring her wishes. That was just like him, to do what he wanted despite what others said. "About your case," he added unnecessarily. Why else would he be pestering her? It wasn't as if he regularly dropped by to visit on a normal day. Normal…the word held no meaning for her now. She couldn't remember *normal* any longer. Maybe she was delirious from lack of sleep. Maybe she was eternally cracked in the head because she couldn't think straight, couldn't think beyond basic needs. And when she said "basic," she meant the very basics.

The slow but steady tug on the blankets caused her to pull harder but her strength was laughable. Tears welled in her eyes as she felt the blanket slip from her grip. All that covered her was the sheet. Sundance stood in a pile of blankets, his gaze alarmed. She imagined she looked frightening. She didn't care. She lifted her chin and met his stare. "What do you want?" she asked dully, wishing to hide but he'd made that impossible. "I said go away."

Sundance had never minced words with her. In all the years she'd known him he'd never held back. To be fair, neither had she. But as he stared at her, his gaze taking in every disgusting detail of her self-imposed retirement from the human race, she saw something different. Uncertainty. She would've rather that he started yelling at her or baiting her than what she saw in his eyes right now. The heavy silence battered at the thin, tattered veil of spunk she had left. Curling in a ball, she turned away from him, shame and defeat coating her every thought. Why'd he have to come? Couldn't he have just left her alone? Had Mya sent him? She couldn't imagine her best friend would betray her this way but, Great Spirit help her, she didn't know what else to think.

"Have you eaten?" he asked.

She thought of the piece of toast she'd forced down, was it yesterday? Or maybe it was the day before that? She answered, "I'm not hungry."

"When was the last time you showered?" It'd been a while. She could smell herself and it wasn't pretty, but there was a small comfort in her own stink. Perhaps if she smelled bad enough no one would come near her. When she didn't answer, he said, "Never mind. I think I can figure that one out on my own. Come on, it's time to get up and get moving again," he announced, the grim tone telling her he wasn't looking forward to the prospect, either.

"Not today," she answered, clutching a pillow to her belly.

"Yes, today," he countered, his firm control back in full swing. He'd always been such a bossy jerk, she

noted almost distantly. "First things first, a shower."
Because you smell, is what he hadn't said but she heard
anyway.

"I don't feel like it. Maybe tomorrow," she said in the
hopes of sending him on his way.

"Today," he repeated, going to her bathroom to start
the water.

"Go to hell," she muttered, but there was little heat
and he called her on it.

"Say it like you mean it or don't waste my time. Now
let's go," he said, his stance hard and unyielding, like
a drill sergeant with an unruly private. "It's time to
get back into the swing of things and that starts with a
shower. We'll work our way up from there."

Her eyes stung. Why wouldn't he go away? "You're
cruel. Don't you understand I can't just yet?"

If there was a softening in his gaze, it was gone in an
instant. "You're giving up. That's not the Iris I know."

She closed her eyes. "That girl is gone."

"No. She's just buried under the layers of stink you're
marinating in. Now, either you can get out of that bed on
your own accord or I can haul you out. It's your choice,
but you'd better do it within the next three seconds or
I'll make the choice for you."

"Go…to…*hell.*" This time she added more heat
as anger started to thaw the frozen tundra filling the
landscape inside her.

He offered a harsh smile. "That's more like it but I
know you can do better. Time's up." He approached her
and she shrieked as she surmised his intent. She kicked
at him but he managed in one fluid movement to rip
her sheet from her body and toss her over his shoulder.
She screamed and pounded his back, tears blinding her.
Panic built until it threatened to choke the air from her

lungs. She inhaled a sharp, painful breath, her mouth working to produce sound but something from her blank memory of that night broke loose and strangled her vocal cords until only a soft mewling escaped her lips. ·

"Don't do this," she gasped, kicking her feet, but he held her securely, thwarting her best efforts, that were pretty pathetic given how weak she felt from not eating or sleeping. "Sonny…please…" she whispered, tears flowing down her cheeks to land on the carpet as he carried her to the bathroom that had filled with steam. "I can't…"

"You can," he disagreed, depositing her in the shower, still clothed in her sleep shirt and underwear. She gasped as the water pelted her. It was at once scalding and soothing. She sobbed, flashes of memory coming to her from that night. She'd sat on the floor of the hospital shower after Mya had examined her, watching as the water washed away the blood and dirt but could do nothing to remove the pain and degradation. She'd remained in that shower until the water ran cold but by that time she'd become numb. That'd been the last time she'd showered. She shuddered as great, racking sobs shook her body. Sundance seemed on autopilot and was unmoved by her total breakdown. He grabbed the shampoo and squirted a modest handful into her shaking hands. "Start with this," he instructed. "I trust you can handle the rest."

And then he left, closing the door behind him. She stared at the green glob in her palm as if it were her enemy. But in truth, the enemy was the sentinel outside her door, demanding she put herself back together.

Damn you, Sundance. I hate you.

If only that were true…maybe none of this would've happened.

Her breath hitching painfully in her chest, she began to scrub until her scalp ached but just as she knew that night…nothing would ever take away the stain of what had been done to her.

Nothing.

Chapter 3

Sundance hands shook as he shoved them through his hair, listening as the water continued to fall in the shower. He knew he was taking a chance pushing her like that, Great Spirit help him, he'd felt each quake of her body against his as true panic had caused her to kick and scratch against his touch. Seeing her shrink into herself, trying to disappear, tore a fissure of wrath and helplessness inside him. But he couldn't allow Iris to fade into nothingness. So if it meant being the coldhearted bastard who forced her to stay with the living, so be it.

Releasing a short, tight breath, he surveyed the room she'd turned into her prison cell and wondered how Iris had managed to live in such conditions. The stale, closed-in air was enough to send a normal person running for the window, which was exactly what Sundance did first. Throwing open the window, not caring that it was a little brisk outside, he started pulling the blankets from the floor to take them to the washing machine. He'd been here with Mya enough times to know the layout of the house but he never imagined he'd find himself actually doing Iris's laundry. Up until recently, he hadn't found much use for Iris aside from her being his sister's best friend.

But things had changed. He wasn't quite sure when or how but they had. Before he'd had time to deal with his feelings, Iris had been attacked.

He made quick work of throwing everything in the washing machine and then returned to make the bed with fresh sheets. Having grown up with alcoholic parents, the responsibility of running the house had often fallen to Sundance. Well before most friends his age, he'd known how to cook, clean and drive. He'd just finished when steam escaped from the door as it opened.

Iris emerged from the bathroom, her long blue-black hair lying limply against the deep, rich burgundy bathrobe, her stare red-rimmed and accusatory as it bounced from the freshly made bed and back to him again. "Why'd you come?" she asked, her lip quivering. She clutched the lapels of her bathrobe closer to her neck as if trying to ensure every square inch of skin was under lock and key. Her desperate movements only accentuated how she'd changed in the course of one damned, ill-fated evening.

Iris had always been proud of her womanly curves, now she was doing everything she could to cover them.

"You can't hide in your house for the rest of your life," he said gravely, meeting her stare for stare, though what he saw reflected in her eyes made him ache for the loss of something he'd never known he'd wanted.

"I'm not hiding."

"Mya says you haven't been to work in weeks and you never leave the house. I'd call that hiding."

"I'm using my vacation and sick days." She swallowed, looking away. "I'm…regrouping." Sundance took a step forward, compelled to reach out to her in some way but she returned the distance between them by taking a faltering step backward until her back bumped against the wall. A hard knot lodged in his chest.

"Iris…" he started but she shook her head.

"I'm fine. It's fine. I just need to be alone for a little while."

She wasn't fine. Any fool could see she was the opposite of the word. Mya had to see her friend was drowning. Why wasn't she making more of an effort to draw Iris out? Surely wilting and withering away in this house wasn't healthy. "I can't let you do this to yourself."

"I'm not doing anything."

"Exactly. Not eating, not showering, not leaving the house. You need to snap out of it."

Her eyes were dry but when he met her gaze he felt waves of grief and shame rolling over him and it made him want to put his fist through the wall. "I'll be fine," she said, nodding.

"Stop saying that," he bit out. "Damn it, Iris, you're not *fine*. You're punishing yourself by barricading yourself up in this house like some kind of communicable disease. It wasn't your fault. Whoever did this is scum, not you. Help me catch this son of a bitch before he does it to someone else."

"I don't remember," she whispered, shaking her head

in a pathetic, scared little rabbit motion that tore at his heart. "I don't remember…I can't help anyone." She pulled the lapels tighter around her body as she began to shudder. "There's a big white spot in my memory and I don't think I want to remember. What if he's someone I know? What if he's watching me all the time, waiting to do it again?"

"That's not going to happen," he said, fighting to keep the growl from his voice. "We're going to catch him."

"You don't know that."

"I know that I won't stop until I do."

She squeezed her eyes shut. "I can't help you. I wish I could. I can't remember. It's safer if I stay in the house. He might know where I work. He might follow me. If I stay here…he won't find me."

He wasn't angry with her but seeing her so broken, so torn apart mentally, it awoke a rage so fierce that he wanted to break things for her sake. But he couldn't do that, not when he needed to keep a calm head in order to catch whoever did this, not when he needed to be the one person in Iris's life to keep her focused and moving forward so that she could get through this. He didn't know why he knew he was the one for the job but he accepted it as he accepted all his responsibilities. He walked slowly to Iris even as she kept her eyes screwed shut. He could see her body quivering through the robe and he didn't know if it was caused by cold or fear. He lowered himself beside her, taking care not to crowd her but close enough to let her know he was there. He'd never been one to coddle people, never been accused of being much of a nurturer. But here, now, he wished he had more of those qualities. He felt ill-equipped to deal with this kind of emotional trauma but he couldn't leave her this way either. They sat in silence for a long while until Sundance recalled a memory from their childhood in the hopes of distracting her.

"Remember that time you hid a dead crawdad in my room and I couldn't find it for weeks?" He smiled at the memory, remembering how bad his room had smelled before he'd found it tucked under his bed. "I'd known it was you even though you denied it. Even swore on your mother's life that it wasn't you. I wanted to kill you for that one." But Mya had pointed out that if he hadn't embarrassed Iris by snapping her bra in front of everyone during lunch recess, she wouldn't have felt compelled to seek revenge. He'd grudgingly let that one slide. But there were countless other times when Iris had been the aggressor, the one who'd purposefully gone out of her way to make his life miserable for the simple pleasure of watching his blood pressure rise. He never thought he'd miss that Iris. But sitting here with that woman's shell was almost too difficult to bear.

"Why are you here?" she whispered.

"Because someone has to be." He looked her over with a clinical eye. There was no hiding the fatigue that bracketed her eyes, the sallow skin that usually glowed with health and vitality. "When was the last time you slept?"

The minute shake of her head told him she couldn't remember. "He's out there. Every time I close my eyes he's there, watching me. Waiting."

"I'm here." No one was going to touch her. He'd make sure of it. He felt pressure against his biceps as she tentatively laid her head against him. "No one's going to touch you."

"So scared…" she admitted in a tight, barely audible voice. "So tired…"

"Then sleep," he instructed softly.

She settled and, after a moment, her breathing became deep and he knew she'd fallen asleep. Pure exhaustion had won out.

Rising carefully, he maneuvered her into his arms and lifted her to the bed. With her eyes closed in sleep, lush lashes resting against her cheeks, and a full mouth that, until recently, he'd always teased her about, calling her fish lips, he found her features familiar yet foreign. Her hair, still wet from the shower, hung down his arm in a fall of black waves that shone like the liquid surface of a lake under the moon's glow. He placed her on the bed and carefully pulled the blankets over her. Satisfied she was warm enough, he went to the window and closed it, not wanting her to catch a chill for the sake of fresh air.

He couldn't bring himself to leave, not until he knew she'd at least slept a full eight hours and eaten a decent meal. If that meant he had to stay until that was accomplished, so be it.

The road to recovery was long, but she wasn't alone. He just had to remind her of that fact.

Iris remembered laughing, enjoying a drink at the bar. The music had been loud and the lights dim. She remembered returning a smile, thinking the guy was good-looking and an excellent specimen for her objective, which had been to get Sundance off her mind. She didn't want to be attracted to her best friend's older brother. She'd known him her entire life, so why now? It was as if a light had been turned on in her head and suddenly she was seeing him in a completely different way. She'd never noticed his lean hips and wide shoulders or the way his mouth gentled when he let his guard down and actually smiled. No, she absolutely hadn't noticed those things. Thank God. Like life wasn't complicated enough?

And yet…

So Operation Distract Yourself had been going well.

In her dream state, memory and fiction blended together to create a nightmarish landscape. Soon, the music blared to the point of creating pain in her ears. The lights strobed in dizzying seizure-inducing patterns and the sudden touch on her arm as she was pulled from the bar seemed welcome at first.

But then the grip tightened like a vise and agony radiated through her body as the hand that had seemed friendly became aggressive and demanding. Her vision was fuzzy and unfocused. She couldn't make out his features but she was nauseated by the blend of malice and excitement washing over her. Hands grabbing, punching, violating…

She slapped at the phantom attacker, a scream caught in her throat, trapped and useless, until the scene shifted with a slow slide to endless black that was somehow less frightening and even soothing.

At least when she was drifting in midnight, no one was hurting her.

Chapter 4

Mya, on break between patients at the clinic, peppered him with questions.

"How'd she seem?" she asked, frowning as if she already knew the answer, which she probably did, and just wanted Sundance to confirm or deny. "She's having a rough time still, isn't she?"

"Yeah, you could say that," he answered drily, still troubled over Iris's departure from the human race. "She's totally cut herself off from everyone and it's not healthy. You of all people should know that. Mya… why haven't you tried to coax her out?" Mya affected a wounded expression and tears welled in her eyes, making him realize he'd totally bungled that one and he tried to make amends. "It's not your fault. I'm sorry. I don't know what's coming out of my mouth. The situation has got me all tied up in knots."

She rested her hand on his shoulder. "I know. And

trust me, I tried. She won't listen and I'm afraid to push her too hard. As a doctor I can be clinical about certain things but she's my best friend and more like a sister. I can't seem to separate my feelings. Any leads on who did this?"

"No," he admitted, frustrated. "But I don't have much to go on with Iris's memory of the event compromised. Have the toxicology reports come back yet?"

"No, but it should be soon," she promised. "I'll call as soon as they do."

"Thanks. Listen, I've got an errand to do before heading back out to Iris's house. I just stopped by to let you know that there's a new guy in town, and before you say you're not interested in meeting anyone, he's not exactly a stranger. He's an old friend of mine named Chad Brown, who's been assigned to the area as the liaison to the Bureau of Indian Affairs."

"And how do you know him?" she asked, her brow lifting with faint interest.

Sundance smiled. "He used to live here. We were friends up until he left in junior high and then we caught up to each other again after high school. He went the college route, while I went law enforcement. He's a good guy. I think you'll like him."

"Any relation to Paul Brown, the director of Indian Affairs?"

"Chad is his son."

"Nice to have connections," Mya quipped.

"In this day and age, it absolutely is. But don't hold the nepotism against him. He's really made a name for himself in certain circles. He's done a lot of good work out there for Native Americans. You could do a lot worse."

"Mmm-hmm," was all she said to that. "I'm a big

girl, Sonny. I don't need you trying to find me a date. I can do that all on my own. Besides, with everything that happened to Iris, I can't even think of dating."

"I'm just saying it'd be nice to know my sister has someone to take care of her if I'm not around."

She leveled a direct look his way. "I can take care of myself. Stop acting like you live in the time of our ancestors when women had to have a man to watch over them. I'm perfectly capable of caring for myself, thank you very much. Now, I have patients to see. Please give Iris a hug for me, and thanks for looking out for her."

"I'm just doing my job," he answered gruffly, not comfortable with the spotlight or the implication that he was doing this out of more than a sense of responsibility to one of his tribe. "But in all seriousness, Chad's a solid guy. Just think about it, okay?"

"I'll keep that in mind," she answered in a tone that Sundance knew to mean she would purposefully forget as soon as he left the building. Mya had given her heart away years ago and she hadn't yet recovered from it being shattered. He had hopes, though, and even if he wasn't what he'd consider a matchmaker of any sort, he never passed up the opportunity to let Mya know what her options were. She waved and disappeared, her break over.

Sundance climbed into his Durango. He had two stops to make before heading out to Iris's house. One for food, another…security.

Iris managed to shower and run a brush through her hair, but she couldn't bring herself to open the drapes or windows. Each time she tried, panic seized her by the throat and choked the breath from her lungs. She huddled in her bed, staring at the window, wishing she had the nerve to open it and breathe the cool, cleansing air, but the thought of being visible to whoever might be out there filled her with immobilizing dread. The feeling of being trapped in her home had begun to manifest but she couldn't bring herself to do anything about it. She couldn't move forward or backward and her impotence was maddening.

A knock sounded at the door and her heart jumped in her chest, banging so hard she thought for sure it might pop free, but when she heard Sundance's voice she released a shaky breath and climbed from the safety of her bed to answer the door.

She couldn't say she was happy to see Sundance two days in a row at her darkest hour but she couldn't rightly say she was disappointed either. Again, she was stuck somewhere in the middle.

Iris opened the door and startled when a large black dog sat beside Sundance, eyeing her with the guileless curiosity only animals and babies possessed. "What…?" She gestured to the animal as she looked to Sundance for the answer. "A dog?"

"A guard dog, specifically." He patted the dog's broad head, his hand firmly on the leash. "Saaski, meet Iris, Iris, this is Saaski. He's a wolf-shepherd hybrid and once he's bonded to you, he'll take someone's head off if they try to touch you without your permission."

Iris stared, unable to believe what Sundance had done. Tears brimmed in her eyes. "You got me a guard dog? Why? I mean…I don't understand…"

"You couldn't sleep because you didn't feel secure. I suspect it'll be a long time before you feel totally safe, but until then, Saaski will do his best to make sure that no one gets near you without a fight."

She swallowed, her gaze reluctantly leaving Sundance's

to look at the dog. His thick, rich coat was as dark as sin with twin, burning coals for eyes. His face held the wise cunning of a wolf but he had the solid, muscular build of a German shepherd. She held out her hand to him and he sniffed at it before taking an exploratory lick. His heavy tail thumped and wagged—the dog equivalent to a "Hey, I like you" greeting—and she smiled for the first time in a long time.

She looked up and Sundance handed her the leash. "Thank you," she said, her voice hardly more than a whisper as gratitude overwhelmed her. How'd he know to do this for her? Why hadn't she thought of it for herself? In the past her schedule didn't lend itself to having much more than a houseplant or two but she knew the moment she looked into Saaski's eyes, she'd do whatever she had to to accommodate her new companion. She didn't doubt that this dog would protect her above all things and it meant more than she could voice that Sundance had done this for her. "Please come in," she said, moving aside so he could enter. "Are you hungry? I have, like, twenty frozen casseroles of some sort that Mya brought. I don't know what they are but I'm sure they're edible."

Sundance closed the door but declined her offer. "I can only stay for a few minutes. The breeder I got Saaski from runs an obedience and defense class in Forks. I want you to take it with Saaski. It'll help you bond with him. Plus, the commands he's been taught are in Navajo, so you'll need to know how to control him using the commands he already understands. He's a young dog still, only a year old, but the breeder said he's smart and with the right training, he'll be better than any house alarm you can buy."

She ran her fingers through Saaski's coarse fur. "Is he housebroken?"

"Well, he's kennel trained and I brought the kennel for you. It's in my Durango."

"He sleeps in a box?" she asked, frowning at the idea of putting this glorious animal in a cage. She shook her head. "He can sleep with me."

The corner of Sundance's mouth lifted as if amused. "Somehow I had a feeling you'd say that. All right, I'll put the kennel in the garage and if you need it, you know where to find it. I also bought a small bag of food to get you through to when you could get to town to buy a larger one."

She chewed her lip, hearing what he wasn't saying. Sooner or later she'd need to step outside of this house, if only to purchase dog food.

Sundance cleared his throat, adding, "But this bag should last you a few days."

So she had a few days to get used to the idea of venturing out on the reservation. The thought gave her an unpleasant chill, but she nodded slowly. Of course Sundance was right, she couldn't hide forever no matter how appealing the thought.

"He's beautiful," she said softly. "What does his name mean?"

"The breeder said it means 'of two worlds.'"

"Appropriate," she murmured, continuing to stroke the dog's fur, blinking back tears. She felt caught between two worlds, too. Her previous world and her reality. She met Sundance's stare and her breath hitched in her chest. What did he see? Did she want to know? She pushed her hair behind her ear, glad for the shower she'd taken this morning. "Sundance…about yesterday…" She stopped, the words seeming to dry up on her tongue. How did one thank another for forcing them to return to the land of the living? It's not as if she and Sundance had been close. Yet, his message had come through loud and clear when she'd managed to effectively block out everyone else, including her best friend.

"Not necessary," he started, but she cut him off with quiet determination.

"It is necessary," she disagreed. "I know I need help. I've seen enough traumatized women in my profession to recognize the signs but I never realized it would be so difficult to pick up the pieces and try to move forward. Each time I thought about dragging myself out of my bed toward reclaiming my life, an overwhelming terror took over and I would end up a shaking, crying mess. It became easier to just accept that inside equaled safety, out there—" she gestured outside "—meant danger." Tears pricked her eyes as she admitted, "I'm such a coward."

"You can get through this," he said, holding her stare without reservation. She saw strength, determination and even a hint of anger in those familiar eyes, and she drew comfort in knowing Sundance was ever the same, even if she had changed irrevocably. "And don't you dare bow your head in shame. You did nothing wrong. Remember that."

Her breath caught and she started to shake her head, a litany of reasons why she was to blame came to her tongue but she swallowed the instant response and jerked a short nod. "I'll try."

He seemed satisfied with her answer and the rigid set of his shoulders softened just a little as if he'd been holding back a tremendous wind at his back, or shielding her from some terrible calamity. Moisture blurred her vision again and she realized tears would never be far from the surface when she dared to broach this subject with him or anyone.

"I'm going to find who did this to you," he assured her in a quiet but hard voice and she didn't doubt his sincerity. Sundance had always borne the weight of his responsibilities with stoic resolve. He was hard as granite, as unrelenting as a puma on the hunt. She held no illusions that he wouldn't turn that focus on her when he felt it was time. And apparently he'd felt the time had come. "Iris, I need a formal statement from you about that night," he said.

A shaky smile from suddenly numb lips formed as she shrugged. "Formal or informal, I've told you everything I remember, which isn't a lot." The memory of someone giving a god-awful rendition of Aerosmith's "Dude Looks Like a Lady" banged around in her head for a moment. She could smell the alcohol that had splashed on the bar, the sour perspiration of too many bodies and the faint scent of something sharp and tangy—cologne perhaps—but then nothing. She cleared her throat when it felt as if something were stuck there. "I'm sorry… it's just blank. The stuff I remember…it's nothing of value."

"Let me be the judge of that."

"Sundance, trust me, there's nothing there unless bad singing can be considered a crime."

His mouth firmed. "Whoever did this to you was in that bar. Someone was watching and waiting for the right person. Did you talk or dance with anyone?"

Sweat popped along her hairline and she wiped at it with shaking hands. Music throbbed in her head, the laughter and alcohol went hand in hand. She'd been having fun. She'd gone alone to The Dam Beaver, the only bar actually on the reservation, not the least bit apprehensive about being by herself for it would've been like being afraid of her local grocery store. "I…I don't remember," she stammered, feeling sick. "There were a lot of people that night. Karaoke. Singing. I was laughing at…someone." She rubbed at her forehead, the nausea rising in her throat. "I was thirsty. It was so hot…I ordered a club soda with lime because I knew I'd have to drive home eventually."

"So you'd stopped drinking at some point. How much had you drank at that point?"

"I was tipsy but not drunk," she answered, trying to remember, though her head had begun to spin. "I can't do this right now. I feel sick," she said, dropping Saaski's leash to run to the bathroom. She slammed the door and put her head in the toilet in just enough time to lose the little food she'd eaten from earlier.

As the heaving subsided, Iris shuddered and rested her forehead on the cold porcelain, devastated by her body's knee-jerk reaction to the trauma she'd been through. She knew she suffered from post-traumatic stress. From a clinical viewpoint she recognized the signs but as the person soaking in her own sweat over a memory flash, she couldn't remain in that detached, clinical state.

She dragged her hand over her mouth and rose on shaky legs to rinse the sour taste away. She stared at the door, knowing Sundance was still out there, waiting for her. Her eyes squeezed shut as she willed strength into her legs, prayed for some semblance of control, and when it didn't happen, she cursed her weakness with all the bitterness she could muster because she was fairly certain she'd never be the same again.

* * *

Sundance winced as he heard her retch from behind the closed bathroom door. The reaction had been almost instantaneous. He felt helpless and useless, standing there with a dog leash in his hand while Iris barfed her guts out over a simple question. He muttered an expletive and Saaski cocked his head at him. Restless with the need to do something productive, he went about the business of filling a bowl of food and water for the dog. Then he went to the Durango and put the kennel in the small garage. As a habit, he did a perimeter check and double-checked the lock on the side door. Satisfied things were secure, he returned to the house to find Iris curled on the sofa, stroking Saaski's fur. She didn't immediately look at him when he walked in—embarrassment, he supposed. Mya was always telling him to be more sensitive.

"You feeling okay?" he asked.

She shook her head, her eyes and cheeks red and splotchy from retching. "Sorry. I didn't mean to disappear on you like that."

"Don't apologize. You've been through a major trauma. Nobody expects you to bounce back immediately. Least of all me."

She looked at him, surprise in her gaze. "Really?"

"Of course."

"Then what's with the dragging me out of bed, bringing me a dog and suddenly caring about my mental health?"

He supposed hers were valid questions. He was acting out of character. He couldn't very well tell her that his head was a muddled mess about certain things. The woman had enough to deal with, she didn't need his drama, too. But if he had the guts, he'd tell her that seeing her so broken made him want to break the law and *nothing* made him want to do that. He wanted to find that rotten SOB and make his life a living hell for what he'd done to her. All the things he prided himself on—being the responsible, dependable one with a cool head—went right out the window when he saw Iris hurt. But hell, no! He couldn't say that because he didn't know what to make of it himself. Looking away, he shrugged in answer. "Maybe I don't like the idea of sparring with an unarmed person."

Recognizing his attempt at a joke, she offered a faint smile. "You always were so competitive."

"And so were you," he countered, wishing her eyes would flare to life with that spark he was accustomed to seeing when she was seriously pissed off or determined to make a situation go her way. Instead they remained defeated and listless. And he didn't know how to fix that. He rubbed at the back of his neck, the frustration getting to him. "Hey, make sure you eat something. Okay?" he said.

"I will," she replied, but he didn't believe her. She sighed in irritation and he welcomed the sound. "I have enough food to feed an army. I'll pick something or else Mya will start an IV drip. Don't laugh, she's actually threatened me."

"Good." He approved of his sister's threat. Iris was fading away and he didn't like that at all. He walked to the door, turning as he let himself out, saying, "Make sure you lock this right after I leave. And if you take Saaski out, keep him on the leash so he doesn't run. He'll need a few days to get used to your place. Best to keep him in the house unless he's needing to relieve himself."

Iris nodded as she rose to follow his instructions. The

door closed behind him and he heard the lock sliding into place. A short but wry smile fitted to his mouth. That right there—Iris doing as she was told—was a surefire sign that she wasn't all there yet. Iris, as a rule, never did as she was told.

Especially when the instruction came from him.

Hard to believe he actually wanted the old Iris back.

Chapter 5

Sundance walked into The Dam Beaver, the place where Iris last remembered being, and after his eyes adjusted to the dim light, he approached the bartender and flashed his credentials.

He'd been here right after the incident with Iris, but he liked to remind people that he was still on the case even if everyone else had moved on in their interest level.

When it had first happened, the talk among the tribe had been about the unexpectedly violent attack but now, it was old news.

"You're killing business," Butch grumbled, leaning against the bar with a frown. A few patrons cast furtive glances Sundance's way as they ambled away. He let them go but he made sure they knew he'd seen them. Butch sighed and grabbed a towel to sop up the wet spots left behind. "What can I do for you?"

"I want to talk to you again about the night one of your patrons was attacked."

"Come on, Sundance," he said, scowling, "how many times do I have to tell you that I don't know anything about no woman getting attacked. Whatever happened to her, happened outside of my place."

Sundance narrowed his stare at Butch. "That night was karaoke. What was the crowd like? Anyone stand out? Maybe someone who wasn't local?"

Butch grumbled under his breath but made a show of searching his memory. Unfortunately, the surly bartender failed to pull anything of value from his brain. He shrugged. "Karaoke always brings in the numbers and it's hard to separate the locals from the off-rez, you know? Besides, I'm too busy slinging drinks to ID every Tom, Dick and Harry who walks in."

Frustration ate at Sundance. "You know it was Iris who was attacked. You've known her since she was a kid. Hell, you probably served her mother back in the day. Doesn't it bother you that whoever did this was in your bar?"

Butch glowered then looked away, shamed. "I'm real sorry she got banged up. She's a good girl. I never had no problems with her."

"Yeah, well, show you care by giving me a bit more cooperation. I'm trying to catch whoever did this to her."

"Can't give you what I don't got," he maintained stubbornly, but when he realized Sundance wasn't going anywhere until he left with something useful, he added, "I'll keep my ear open for anything. People start to drinking, their mouths start to flapping. Maybe someone saw something. I'll let you know if anything important comes up."

Sundance handed him a card. "You do that." He turned and surveyed the motley group huddled in small clusters. Given that it was midday, the place was nearly empty. He could imagine how quickly it filled at night. No doubt Butch Jones enjoyed the monopoly of having the only bar on the reservation. He'd have to return on a karaoke night to see what kind of crowd the bar attracted. He'd never been a fan of karaoke himself. Mya had tried to talk him into giving it a try, simply for the entertainment value, but Sundance didn't believe in "letting his hair down" as Iris had put it one time when she'd accused him of being as rigid as an oak. He failed to see how listening to a bunch of tone-deaf drunks doing their best to murder their favorite songs was good fun. He'd rather spend the time fishing or camping. Alone.

He left the bar and headed for the cramped building he called an office that also served as a detainment center/jail for anyone on the reservation who got caught breaking the law. Since the reservation was so small, he was a one-man army as far as law enforcement went and he took that responsibility seriously. He knew the troublemakers and the ones who were harmless nuisances. He also knew who to keep a firm hand on to keep from going bad. And not having a clue as to who had nearly killed Iris in such a brutal attack kept him up at night.

He pulled up and saw Chad Brown waiting for him. Chad hailed him with a wave and a friendly smile, that he returned. "I figured if I waited long enough you'd come along eventually," he said. "Just thought I'd stop by and say hello. I had a few free minutes in between running errands."

"You settling in okay? Not getting lost or anything, are you?" he teased his friend.

Chad chuckled. "It's good to see some things don't change. It feels good to prowl around the old stomping grounds. Weird, but good. I'd have thought there'd been some things that were different but, nope, everything looks the same. Down to the cracked wallpaper in the men's bathroom of The Dam Beaver. Damn, doesn't Butch know that's unsanitary?"

Sundance laughed. "I try not to frequent the bar if I can help it. You might try it."

"Quite possibly excellent advice, but I think drinking at home alone says something about you, doesn't it?" Chad winked.

Sundance laughed and gestured to the station. "Come on in, I'll show you around, not that the tour is extensive or anything. It'll take all of five minutes and that's if I draw it out and show you the backyard."

"Hey, at least that's five minutes not spent being my dad's errand boy, so I'm game."

Sundance chuckled. He didn't know the Director of Indian Affairs well—he was just a kid when they'd lived on the reservation—but he'd heard through other channels he was a bit of a bear most times. He supposed working for him—family or not—was probably a major pain in the butt. Sundance went to his minifridge and offered Chad a soda. "Root beer or cola. Sorry no alcohol. Pick your poison."

"I'm a root beer man," Chad answered with good humor, accepting the cold beverage. He cracked it and took a good slug. "So, what's it like being the law here?"

Sundance shrugged, cracking his own soda. "It's honest work. So, what can I do for you?" he asked.

Chad smiled. "Still, the same old Sundance…to the point. Well, here goes…as you know, my father has given me the title of reservation liaison, that means absolutely nothing in terms of pay grade but means he gets to stay hobnobbing with the bigwigs and I get to do all the travel. I wondered if you might help me get to know the community again so that I'm not a total outsider. I don't think anyone but you remembers me from when I was a kid."

"You'd be surprised. Memories are long here," Sundance said, adding with mock seriousness. "That, for you, might not be a good thing. Remember that time you shaved Miss Mamie's cat? Yeah, well, she's still alive and there's nothing wrong with her memory."

Chad shuddered. "Damn, she must be a fossil by now. All right, I'll just take my chances on my own then. Some friend you are," he said with a snort.

"Hey, don't blame me. I told you not to shave that cat. You didn't listen. That's your cross to bear."

"Well, if that's the least of my crimes around here, I'm a lucky son of a bitch."

"Of that, I have no doubt." Sundance smiled, their banter reminding him of when he'd visited Chad in their wild days after high school. They'd lost track of each other for a while but they'd found each other again and it felt the same as before. That was the mark of a true friendship in Sundance's opinion. "All right, getting back to your original request, nothing is going to make the tribe budge faster than good, honest work."

"Bring it on," Chad said. "My back is strong and my hands able."

"Good to know, but in the meantime, let's see how well you take notes. There's an issue that's been shoved under the carpet for too long and it's coming to a head.

It'd be nice to know the tribe had a voice at the Bureau of Indian Affairs."

"I'm your man," Chad said. "What's going on?"

"There's going to be a meeting tonight over at the Tribal Center about the flood situation facing some of our tribal members. Their ancestral land is being eaten up by the encroaching waters of the Hoh River. We've been asking for federal funds to relocate some of the homes in the worst areas of the flood plain."

"And let me guess, you're getting stonewalled…"

"You got it."

Chad rubbed his hands together. "I love a project. Count me in."

Sundance grinned. The man had enthusiasm. That counted for something in his book. "See you at six o'clock then?"

"You bet."

His radio went off and CeCe, his dispatcher, said, "Sonny, you'd better head over to Bunny's place. Sounds like things are getting heated and you know how he gets when he's had too much drink."

That he did. William "Bunny" Roberts, like about half the population of the reservation, was out of a job and he self-medicated his depression with plenty of alcohol. Sundance often had to take Bunny in on domestic charges because the man wasn't exactly soft and cuddly when he was in this kind of state. "Copy that," he answered into the radio. He returned to Chad. "Duty calls. See you tonight?"

"I wouldn't miss it."

Chad followed him outside the building and Sundance locked up. He didn't wait to see where Chad went from there, he had more important things to do. Like keeping Bunny from pissing off his wife so much that she blew his head from his shoulders with that 12-gauge shotgun Sundance wasn't supposed to know about.

Iris wasn't surprised when Mya showed up on her doorstep later that evening after the clinic had closed. She suspected Mya had been after Sundance for details and now that Iris was no longer petrified to leave her bed, she probably figured it was safe to visit.

She opened the front door and found Mya bearing food—as usual—however, this time, Iris offered a genuine smile and invited her in to stay for a while. She'd missed Mya but she hadn't realized just how much until she read the relief in her best friend's eyes.

"You look better," Mya said, trailing behind Iris as they walked to the kitchen so Iris could dish up the casserole Mya had brought. "How are you feeling?"

Ever the doctor, Iris mused silently. She smiled. "Healing, I guess," she answered.

It'd been almost four weeks since the attack. The worst of the bruising had faded to a pale and sickly yellow but at least the swelling had gone away. There remained one thing she needed to fully put the situation behind her and she wouldn't get that for a few more days. Mya surmised the direction of her thoughts and said quietly, "The morning-after pill should have prevented… anything from…"

Iris risked a tremulous smile. Great Spirit forgive her, but she hoped and prayed every day that whoever had attacked her hadn't planted a baby in her womb. She wanted babies someday but not like this. "I know. It's okay." She choked down a lump and forced the tears from her eyes. Iris wasn't going to waste her visit with Mya on crap like this. For heaven's sake she just wanted to feel normal again. And that included indulging in conversation that wasn't weighted by sadness and grief. She wiped at her eyes and handed Mya a plate that she almost refused but Iris wasn't about to eat alone. She'd had enough of that. "Come on now, you brought enough food to feed the entire tribe. The least you could do is sit with me and enjoy it."

Mya's smile widened with joy. "I'd be happy to."

They spent the next hour eating and enjoying each other's company in a basic bid to reconnect after a horrible tragedy.

Iris hugged Mya and held her tight. "Thank you," she whispered, tears leaking down her face. "I'm sorry for locking you out."

"Don't apologize," Mya said fiercely. "I wasn't going anywhere. I was just waiting until you were ready."

They broke the embrace and Iris wiped at her eyes. She had Sundance to thank for dragging her into the present. Saaski wandered in from her bedroom to settle at her feet. Mya's eyes widened at the sight of the dark, dangerous-looking dog. "Oh, my, is that…?"

Iris laughed and leaned down to scratch between Saaski's ears. "Yes, my new personal security system. Isn't he beautiful?"

"Beautiful, yes. Scary, absolutely," Mya said, eyeing Saaski with a bit of fear. "Wherever did Sundance find such a dog?"

Iris shrugged. "I don't know. He said he knew the breeder."

"A regular dog wouldn't have done the trick?" Mya asked.

"Sundance must've known I needed something with bite. He's perfect," she said with admiration, suddenly clarifying, "the dog, not Sundance."

"I know what you meant." Mya pushed her plate away

and rose to clear the dishes. There was more than her mild concern over Iris's new dog reflecting in her eyes, and Iris had a feeling it wasn't good news.

"Out with it, Jonson. You're terrible at keeping secrets," Iris said, half joking. "Whatever it is, I can handle it."

Mya flashed a pained smile and Iris loved her all the more for her desire to shield her from whatever was weighing on her mind. "The toxicology results came in right as I was leaving the office." Iris held her breath and waited. Mya sighed unhappily, continuing, "Your blood tested positive for ketamine."

"That accounts for the memory loss," Iris murmured, her dinner sitting like lead in her stomach. "What else did you find?"

Mya shook her head. "Not much. DNA analysis came back negative for matches."

"So basically, aside from the drug he used, we've got nothing useful to catch this person?" At Mya's nod, Iris swore softly but otherwise tried to keep a level head, which was near impossible when inside she was screaming. "Well, that's the way it goes, I guess."

Chapter 6

He'd always been attracted to Indian women. He loved the feel of their thick, dark hair fisted in his hand, loved the way their dark eyes filled with fear when they realized what he was going to do to them. There was nothing to compare to the thrill of the chase and the inevitable capture.

Iris Beaudoin had been smoother than fine liquor.

He replayed in his mind the first moment he'd seen her from across the crowded bar. She'd been wearing a tight V-neck top that had hugged her big breasts in a way he appreciated. It was as if she'd worn that particular top just for him. Her long, black hair had hung down her back, curling in lazy ripples that tempted him in the worst way. Her eyes had danced, her thirst for life evident in the way her confident smile had drawn every man from the bar. He'd known right away, she was for him. He'd wanted to drink her in until she was dry. He could still see the way the curve of her waist had flared to generous hips, could feel his hands clutching those hips as he pounded into her soft, helpless body.

He shuddered at the memory, blood rushing to his groin.

Of all his girls, Iris had been the sweetest, most satisfying. Maybe because even drugged out of her mind, she'd tried to fight. The rest had just lain there like broken rag dolls, their heads lolling to the side, drool escaping their slack mouths, as he'd violated them in every way he could imagine.

But not Iris. She'd made him work for his prize. And what a prize it was. It was enough to make him want a second go round. He'd never been interested in a girl he'd already had but Iris was different. She was in his blood. And he wanted more.

He lifted a Ziploc bag with a pair of white silky panties inside from his secret box and after carefully bringing the scrape of material to his nose, he inhaled deeply, finding extreme pleasure in the faint scent that had remained.

Ahhh, Iris. Still his favorite.

He replaced his treasure and tucked it among his others, inordinately pleased to see how his treasure trove had grown over the years. And no one suspected….

Sundance glowered at the slip of paper in his hand, wishing something—anything—had come up in the DNA analysis that would lead to the man who'd raped Iris, but he was staring at a big fat zero. He met Mya's stare. "Iris already know?"

"I told her last night," she admitted. "It was after hours when the fax came through and I thought she ought to hear first. I'm sorry."

He waved away her apology, knowing Mya was just looking out for Iris. "She okay?" he asked, afraid the knowledge might send Iris into a backslide.

"She's doing as well as can be expected." Mya smiled. "She loves the dog, by the way."

He allowed a short smile as a tendril of warmth tickled his breastbone. "Yeah? I thought she would. The minute I saw the dog, I knew it was the one for Iris."

"Where'd you find a half-wolf hybrid breeder?" she asked.

"A search warrant for something else. Long story short, the breeder owed me a favor and since most people want puppies, he was more than happy to offload Saaski for a good price."

"Are you sure he's safe? He looks vicious."

"He's what Iris needs. Something that makes her feel safe. A Chihuahua wasn't going to get the job done. If anyone tries to come near Iris who seems threatening in any way, he'll—"

"Eat them?"

He grinned. "*Deter* them."

Mya digested the information and then cocked her head to the side assessing him openly. He shifted under her gaze. She had an uncanny way of seeing through him, had since they were kids. This was no different, especially when she said, "You don't have to pretend that you don't care about her. I've known for a while that your feelings had changed about Iris."

"Don't make more out of this than it is," he warned, uncomfortable with how close to home Mya was hitting. "I got the woman a dog. I would've done the same for anyone in the tribe."

"But it wasn't just anyone. It was Iris. And if this

hadn't happened to her, things between you might've been able to take their course naturally."

Maybe. Maybe not. He and Iris were like fire and ice. Even if Iris hadn't been attacked, he doubted either was going to undergo a rapid personality change to suit the other. Iris was as difficult as he was stubborn. He didn't see how the two character traits meshed together to create anything more than a chaotic mess. "How's she doing?" he asked, changing the focus. "Think she might be able to return to work soon?"

"I don't know. She's still pretty shaken up. She's trying to bounce back, but it's like watching someone try to piece together a broken vase with only half the pieces. I could sure use the help, though. The clinic has been filled to capacity and the nurse brought in to cover for Iris just isn't the same. She tends to get flustered with our caseload," she admitted.

"I think she ought to get back to work as soon as possible. It might take her mind off things."

"Maybe, but burying herself in work is just the same as hiding in her house. They're both exercises in avoidance."

"She takes pride in her work. She needs something to rebuild her confidence, to help her rediscover her center. She can't do that from inside her house."

Mya nodded, seeing his point. "I'll talk to her, see what she says. How was the meeting last night? I couldn't seem to get out of here on time."

Sundance sighed, annoyance ripping through him at the memory. "Same as usual. We talked, no one on the federal level listened. There was a lot of commiseration but no action. The tribe is going to drown in the Hoh before they do something about it."

Mya looked troubled. "And what did they say about your request for another tribal officer?"

He couldn't keep his frustration from his voice as he answered tersely, "My request was shot down. They said since the reservation is only one square mile, it didn't justify the need for another officer."

"Our population has exploded. You're constantly running from one call to the next," Mya said with growing anger. "Damn the bureaucrats who won't see what's going on down here. Do you think it would help if I told them how our clinic is nearly bursting at the seams with patients?"

"I doubt it, but you might want to sit down and talk with Chad Brown. You know, that guy I told you about earlier?"

"And why would I want to chat with him?"

"Chad was at the meeting last night and he's jumping in with both feet on the issues. I think we might have an advocate where it counts."

"That'd be a first." Mya nodded, but there was a wariness to her stare as she said, "I'll do what I can to help, but this better not be some kind of ploy to get me to see him as a romantic possibility. You're a terrible matchmaker, so I'd advise you to stick to what you're good at, my brother."

Sundance scowled, clearly caught. "It's time you move on, sis."

She stiffened but forced a smile. "I have nothing to move on from. This isn't about Angelo. It's about my work and how busy I am. I truly don't have time to date right now. Okay? So stop worrying."

Easier said than done. Angelo Tucker had done a number on his sister years ago, and despite her protests to the contrary, Sundance felt she still nursed that particular wound. Why else would a beautiful, successful, spirited and strong woman remain unattached? His thoughts skipped to Iris and he was irritated with himself at how quickly his heart rate jumped at just the thought of her. Iris Beaudoin had never felt compelled to be attached to any one person but not because she'd been burned in the past. She just liked her freedom, or at least that's how it appeared. Now…a pang of anguish followed. No one deserved what had happened to Iris. He had to find who'd done this terrible thing, or else each time he saw Iris he'd see how he failed.

Today Iris was venturing out.

She blew out a short breath and focused on settling the rapid, staccato beat of her heart and ignoring the screech of terror that sounded in her mind when she stepped over the threshold and whistled for Saaski to come. As soon as the dog bounded to her side, his sable coat gleaming in the bright sunlight, her heart rate calmed and her panic ebbed. She swallowed and headed for her rugged, older model Bronco. The '88 Ford had a lot of miles but it was tough and strong and she needn't worry about dog hair on the upholstery. She opened the door and Saaski, after a moment's hesitation, jumped into the driver's seat. "You're the passenger, buddy," she informed him, giving him a helpful nudge so she could climb in.

For a long moment she sat in the Bronco, her keys clutched in her hand. Her Bronco had been left behind at The Dam Beaver. Whoever had taken her had used his car to leave the bar. Mya had driven Iris's vehicle home after Sundance had given the all clear. She hadn't been behind the wheel since that night. Saaski, sensing her distress, whined and pawed at the window. Wiping at the moisture in her eyes, she reached over and rolled the window down far enough for some air flow but not enough for Saaski to jump out. She didn't know how well he traveled just yet. She was about to find out.

"Let's go talk with this breeder of yours. He's going to teach me some Navajo, and you and I are going to become very good friends. Sound like a plan?"

Saaski gave a doggie grunt and his tongue lolled.

"I'll take that as a yes," Iris said, gunning the engine. The rumble of the Ford was soothing even if her hands shook on the steering wheel. "No more hiding…no more fear," she murmured with conviction. "A journey starts with one step."

Perhaps if she said it enough times, she'd believe it.

Once she pulled onto the highway, cranked the radio and started singing, her panic had subsided and it felt good to be out and about. She glanced at Saaski and smiled. Sundance had been right—the dog helped.

Chapter 7

A full month after she'd been attacked, Iris finally returned to work. Mya was, of course, relieved, but there was worry, too. Iris knew her well enough to peel away the layers of her best friend's relief to the bare concern beneath.

"I'm fine," Iris assured Mya for the tenth time, and she was actually starting to believe it…as long as she didn't think too hard about what she couldn't remember. Her period had come and gone, relinquishing the last hold on her ability to move on and she was ready to put it all behind her. "I need to work. Besides, my house is too small to remain in 24/7. There are only so many projects I can start and not finish in one lifetime," she joked, referencing her penchant for being a great starter but not so great of a finisher when it came to hobbies. She had countless half-finished projects throughout her house, from paint jobs to mosaic tile work—she liked the idea of creating something from sweat equity, but not so much of the actual follow-through. "Besides, I heard you were going crazy with your new nurse. Let's face it, there's only one of me—making me irreplaceable."

Mya teared up and threw her arms around Iris, shocking her with the sudden action. "You *are* irreplaceable," she agreed with a watery sniff. "It's been a mess without you." She pulled away and wiped at her eyes, her cheeks red. "I'm sorry. I'm just so happy to have you back but I don't want you to do anything you're not ready for."

"I'm ready to think of something other than myself," Iris shared quietly. "Within my four walls, there's only me. It was nice enough when I was unable to face the idea of being out and about but once that passed, it became a prison. I love my house but I don't want to be on house arrest."

Mya nodded. "I hear you. Okay…well, then we're happy to have you back. I should warn you…the charts are a mess and the scheduling has been back-to-back. We haven't had a dull moment since you left. You're going to have to jump back in with both feet and start running because it's nonstop."

Iris grinned. "Just the way I like it, chaotic and going full tilt. Bring it on, Doc." Mya returned the smile and Iris thought she ought to add, "Oh, one other thing… Saaski is in the break room, so don't be alarmed if you see a devil dog lounging on the sofa."

Mya's grin faltered. "Inside?"

"Well, I couldn't very well leave him at home. He goes with me wherever I go."

Mya nodded, reluctantly agreeing, and saying with a sigh, "Just don't let him eat any of the staff. We have a hard enough time getting qualified people here as it is."

"No worries. He's on a strict no-people-unless-they're-bad diet."

"Fabulous." Mya slipped on her lab coat and disappeared to start the day.

Iris smoothed her scrubs, enjoying the familiar feel of the cotton beneath her palms. Before, she'd never given things like her routine much thought. Now, she was thankful for each day, each moment that felt normal.

A small bead of perspiration dotted her hairline as she fought the sour lump of apprehension that followed the realization that she would be facing the community again—baring herself to their scrutiny and their questions. She could do this. First and foremost, she was a professional health care giver. Keep the chatter to a minimum, she instructed herself. That way she communicated without words that she wasn't interested in satisfying everyone's morbid curiosity. She was alive—that's what mattered—and she had a job to do.

As the sun sank into the horizon, signaling an end to the day, Sundance made his way over to the Healthy Living urgent care center. Mya had told him it was Iris's first day back at work and he thought he'd swing by and see how it went, it would also enable him to broach a different subject.

He wanted Iris to see a forensic hypnotherapist to see if a professional could unlock her memory of the attack. He expected a refusal but he had to try.

Iris and Saaski exited the back door and he was pleased to see Saaski responding well to her commands. The two were a good fit together. Iris opened her Bronco and Saaski jumped in. She'd just taken her seat when he approached the vehicle.

"How was the first day?" he asked, making conversation. It struck him as odd that before the incident, he would've never thought to strike up pointless banter with the woman. If he'd needed to speak with her, he would've gotten straight to the point. Now, he felt compelled to chat first.

Iris rubbed at her eyes, no doubt tired, and nodded as she answered with a yawn. "Satisfying. Felt good to do something useful."

"Mya missed you," he said. "She didn't want to hurt anyone's feelings but she was a bit underwhelmed by the quality of your replacement."

"She's just used to my style because we've been working together for so long. I'm sure it would've been fine," she murmured, but he could tell she enjoyed being so valued. And he didn't see anything wrong with that. He'd never had any complaint about her work ethic. "You know, I never got a chance to thank you properly for bringing me Saaski. He's a great dog."

He allowed a short smile, heat flooding his chest at her admission. "You sleeping again?" he asked gruffly.

"Like a baby," she answered, smiling. "Anyway, I know you're not one for sentimental gibberish but it meant a lot to me that you cared. We haven't always been...*friendly* to each other, but you were a real friend when you brought me Saaski. So...thank you."

"I would've done it for anyone," he said. "The tribe's safety is my responsibility."

"Ah, of course," she said, withdrawing a bit. "The tribe has always been your priority. Guess I'm glad I fall under that umbrella."

Her wounded reaction made him want to apologize but he wasn't sure what he was apologizing for. He only knew that he wanted to wipe away that expression, even if he wasn't sure why. The best thing would be to focus on the job at hand, he counseled himself when the awkward silence stretched between them. "Listen…I wondered if you'd be willing to see a hypnotherapist— one that specializes in memory retrieval." He threw the request out there, not surprised when she shut down.

"Not interested," she replied, sticking her key in the ignition and firing up the Ford. "Just let it go, okay? I don't really want to know what happened. We both know the outcome of the evening, I don't need details. Maybe it's a blessing in disguise that I can't remember."

"What if it happens to someone else?" he asked.

"The odds are slim. It was probably just someone passing through. I'm ready to put it behind me and I can't do that if I'm reliving the experience in full Technicolor."

He understood but the key to solving the case was locked in her head, he could feel it. "Iris, don't you want closure?" he asked.

She met his stare without reservation and said, "That's what I'm doing. I'm working on closure. This is my way of putting it behind me. I'm sorry, Sundance. I can't. I won't. I'm done and moving on."

Sundance stepped away from the Bronco so she could pull away. Frustration gnawed at him. He sensed something bad was in the air. His great-grandmother used to say that when the spirits were restless, something bad was coming. And he felt it all around him, a sense of malice hanging in the air, draping over the tribe like a blanket of danger.

But he could tell Iris wasn't going to budge. He

couldn't exactly blame her—he could follow her logic quite easily—but the awful sense of responsibility weighing him down refused to let it ride.

Somehow he had to convince her to change her mind before someone else fell victim to whoever had attacked Iris.

He shook off the shudders that tripped along his spine and tightened his jacket around his neck as a frigid wind signaled rain on the way.

Yes…something bad was coming. Or maybe it was already here.

Sierra Buck was an exceedingly pretty young intern at the Tribal Center where she filed papers, typed emails and sorted mail as part of her work experience credit at the high school.

She had a blinding smile that stopped anyone who happened to get caught in her field of vision and generally speaking, everyone liked her for her amiable disposition.

And she'd caught his eye.

At sixteen, Sierra was a little young for his current tastes but he was willing to make an exception for exceptional people.

The dilemma, of course, was how to get her into his possession. The usual bar routine certainly wouldn't work, as she was too young to drink and he couldn't very well cart her off in his car as she'd likely scream her bloody head off before the ketamine kicked in. He couldn't have that.

But he enjoyed a challenge and since he was in need of a new diversion, he happily accepted the challenge of young Sierra Buck.

He played a dangerous game but that was part of

the thrill. To be right under their noses and yet, walking free.

Sierra…a lovely name. Wouldn't it be sweet if she were a virgin? It'd been a while since he'd had one of those…back to the first. Virgins in bars were hard to find, though, in this day and age. So while he enjoyed the thought of breaking in young, nubile girls, he had to limit that particular delight as the prep work was so tediously exhausting.

However, he was due a treat.

And Sierra looked…delicious.

Iris had lied. She didn't sleep like a baby, though the comforting warmth of Saaski's big body taking up space on her bed helped her to relax a bit. She drowsed in fits and starts, getting snatches of sleep but not truly great stretches of quality REM time. She told herself she needed time. Eventually, she'd get over this but something in the back of her mind resisted the effort she made to comfort herself.

What if she never truly got over it? Would she ever lose this feeling of being forever soiled and stained? It didn't matter how hard she scrubbed her skin, the phantom of her attacker's touch haunted her even if she didn't recall details. She knew what the aftermath had felt like.

Her body had healed, her psyche had not.

She wished she'd had the courage to tell Sundance what had prompted her ill-fated karaoke night but she couldn't. Not now. What man would possibly want her? And how could she fathom letting a man touch her without shuddering in revulsion? A single tear escaped and slid down her cheek as waves of shame and insecurity followed. Saaski, sensing her pain, licked her hand. She smiled and patted his big head.

What if Sundance was right and someone else ended up victimized by the same man? Was she being selfish in refusing to do whatever she could to remember details? Maybe he was right and the identity of her attacker was hidden in her brain. She snuggled further into the blankets, listening to the rain as it pelted the rooftop, her thoughts troubled and heavy.

Chapter 8

Sundance muttered a nasty expletive but tried to keep his cool.

"This isn't right," he said, staring at Chad, trying to comprehend the nonsense he was hearing.

"I know, it's ridiculous," Chad agreed, frowning in tandem with Sundance. "I'm on your side, completely. I can't imagine what they're thinking but I heard that your department is on the chopping block."

"Department?" he exploded, unable to hold back even when he should. "I have a dispatcher who works out of her own home because there's no room at my station and I'm a department of one to handle all calls from domestic violence to poachers. I'm a beat cop and a fish and game warden all in one package and just when I've been trying to convince the feds I need help, they want to cut me?"

"Yeah, it's crazy. I tried to talk some sense into my

old man but he's a bureaucrat and he's all about making himself look good. But it's not a done deal so don't start looking for a new job just yet."

"Then get your old man down here and I'll tell him to his face that he's a damn idiot for not seeing what's in black and white and plain as day if he just took the time to see what's going on here," Sundance shot back, fuming.

Chad chuckled as if the idea of Sundance bawling out his father amused him but he shook his head. "That's not going to win you any points. And points you need," Chad reminded Sundance. "We'll get this figured out. Don't worry."

But that was the thing, Sundance *was* worried. "What do they propose to do when there's an incident on the reservation? This is tribal land. We're entitled to our own police force. This is utter bull," he said, so hot he could barely see straight. If he were thinking with a cooler head he'd realize it was probably idle chatter and highly unlikely to turn into anything serious, but deep down he was sick inside at the thought of leaving his tribe unprotected. An outsider wouldn't care about the real issues facing the tribe, nor would they understand the residents of the small reservation. It was a catastrophe waiting to happen.

Chad ushered him into his office and closed the door. "Here's the thing, I'm your advocate. I will do whatever I can to show my dad and his cronies that this is an ill-advised idea but I need you to put together some numbers. You have to show them that you need more help with hard evidence of the crime levels you're facing and I'm not just talking about the petty stuff. I mean the real violent crimes."

"We don't have a lot of violent crime," Sundance

said, thinking. The incident with Iris had been a terrible shock. "But we have a little bit of everything…more than one person can possibly handle without backup or help."

"Well, what about that case with that nurse?" Chad asked. When Sundance just looked at him, he said, "Well, that sounded pretty serious from what I heard. Maybe she could give testimony or something to the need for police services."

"She's been through enough. I'm not dragging her through some dog and pony show. I'll find something else to convince them."

Chad seemed to realize Sundance was touchy when it came to the subject of Iris and backed off. "Okay, well, put your thinking cap on then because this is serious. The slice of fed pie is shrinking every day and trust me, you're not the only tribe eyeing that pie."

Sundance glanced out the glass window fronting the lobby and caught sight of Sierra Buck—a girl he'd known since she was a baby—chatting with someone he didn't recognize. He gestured with a narrowed stare. "Who's that Sierra is talking to? I don't know him."

Chad frowned and followed his stare before chuckling. "Easy, boy. That's Brett Duncan, the new grant guy. My father said I could bring in someone to help look for funds that could be used to pay for relocation costs for the tribe. He's totally harmless, trust me. He has very good references. Supposed to be some kind of whiz when it comes to grants."

Be that as it may, Sundance was wary of outsiders on the reservation. Especially when one of them was quite obviously flirting with a sixteen-year-old girl. "How old is he? Married? Where's he from?"

Chad shook his head with a smile. "The badge never

comes off, does it?" When Sundance simply stared, Chad lifted his hands in mock surrender and said, "All right, calm down. I have his information right here." He grabbed a file and opened it. "Graduated from Oregon State with a bachelors degree in finance, married to a perfectly lovely wife of three years, and he enjoys chess and Spanish wines. As I said, harmless but incredibly smart and I think he's the tribe's best shot at nabbing additional funds."

"So why's he flirting with a teenage girl if he's happily married?"

"Nothing wrong with flirting, just touching, right?" he joked, but Sundance didn't find it funny. Chad sobered. "All right. I'll have a talk with him, remind him to be mindful of the rules. Sierra is a great girl and I don't want to lose her."

"How long she been working here?"

"She started last week. Some kind of work experience program with the high school. She's doing a bang-up job. I feel terrible that we're paying her slave wages but she doesn't seem to mind."

"Jobs are hard to come by for adults much less the teens around here," Sundance acknowledged grudgingly. He was overreacting but he couldn't shake this feeling of something bad coming and it was driving him crazy. He forced himself to relax and even managed to shoot Chad a short smile. "Just see to it that he remembers she's a kid and treats her like he would his own baby sister…or daughter."

Chad mock saluted him. "You got it, *Capitan*."

Sundance's radio went off at his hip and his dispatcher came on line.

"Got another altercation over at Bunny's house. Sounds serious. He's brandishing a weapon this time."

"Copy that. I'm on my way." He clapped Chad on the shoulder in silent show of *See? What did I tell you?* and let himself out.

As he climbed into his Durango he realized it felt good to have someone on his side, a friend.

But he didn't feel good about this Brett Duncan character. Anyone who would openly flirt with a teenage girl wasn't worth much in Sundance's book.

He was going to keep an eye on that one.

The following day Iris took advantage of the rare break in the rain that was a constant companion to this particular Washington coastline to eat her lunch outside with Saaski. She was midway through her sandwich when Mya found her.

"I see great minds think alike," Mya said, smiling as she copied Iris and spread out a large garbage bag along the bench so as not to get wet. Iris grinned and bit into her sandwich. Mya popped her juice and took a deep swig with a relieved sound. "That hits the spot," she said with breathy appreciation while Iris continued to eat in amusement. "So, how are you? We're not running you ragged on your first week back, are we?"

"Nothing I can't handle," Iris assured her, finishing up and tossing her trash. "Feels good to be useful again. Glad to see not much has changed while I was gone." She scratched the top of Saaski's head. "I missed this... you know, the simple routines I used to take for granted, like, eating a sandwich under the trees behind the clinic. I've done this a hundred times and never given it much thought. I realized I took a lot for granted."

Mya nodded in understanding but there was sadness there, too. Iris knew that the sadness was for her. Iris reached over and grasped her friend's hand. "I'm okay," she said. "I mean, I'm not doing cartwheels but each day gets a little better."

Watching Mya's expression lose some of its tension made the lie worth it. She wasn't okay. She was far from it, but she wasn't going to burden Mya with her problem when she had enough on her plate running the clinic with its overload of patients and not enough staff.

"Sundance tells me he would like you to see a hypnotherapist," Mya ventured, causing Iris to stiffen involuntarily. Mya noted her reaction and surmised, "You're not open to it, are you?"

The question was rhetorical but Iris felt the need to explain, even if the words were painful to admit. "I'm thankful for the blank spots. I can't imagine how much worse this would be if I knew in full detail all that had happened to me. I know it must've been horrific because the very idea of it makes me shake but I've been spared the full reel and I'm good with that. Going to a hypnotherapist might dredge up the memory and I'm not ready for that. I might never be ready. I know Sundance doesn't understand but that's how I feel."

"He doesn't mean to be pushy," Mya said apologetically and Iris didn't hold it against her. Mya and her brother had always been close; it was something she'd secretly envied. She'd grown up alone with an alcoholic mother. A story that was all too common on the rez. "He just wants to catch whoever did this to you."

Iris barked a short, mirthless laugh. "Yeah, I know. He's all about catching the bad guy at whatever cost. Everyone knows he takes his job as the tribal police officer quite seriously. I'm sorry I'm not going to be able to accommodate him in his quest for a perfect record."

Mya frowned. "That's not why he wants to catch

this person. He wants to catch who hurt you," she said reproachfully, adding, "And it's not because you're a tribe member."

Iris met Mya's stare. "What then?"

"Because he cares for you."

"No, he cares for the tribe. Me...he tolerates. It's always been that way, Mya. I've always known it, too. And that was fine with me because frankly I tolerated him, too."

"Iris, you know that's not true. He's always cared about you. And that night? I saw murder in his eyes. He wanted to kill whoever had hurt you. Sonny is always a cool head in a crisis but there was a wildness to him that night...as if the bear spirit had roared inside him. He would've torn that person limb from limb if he'd known who to put his hands on. The only other person he'd protect with his life like that is me."

Iris felt moisture pricking her eyes even as she denied what Mya was saying. "He'd do that for anyone in the tribe. He was doing his job."

Mya sighed and the moment stretched out between them. Mya knew her well enough to know that Iris was digging her heels in and unlikely to budge on this score. She'd seen and heard Sundance defending his actions as something he would do for anyone. She wasn't about to read more into it than that. Besides, it wasn't as if she had a lot to offer. She was buried under layers of grief, anger and humiliation. Anything she could offer another person would be a shadow of her true self and Sundance needed a full-blooded woman, someone who would stand up to him and refuse to back down simply because he glowered at her.

"Sonny...he bears a lot of responsibility and he has always sacrificed his personal feelings and needs for the good of someone else. But I know my brother and he feels something more than friendship or tribal loyalty for you."

A spasm of pain almost caused her to grip her chest for fear she was having a heart attack. "Mya…please…I don't want to talk about this anymore," she pleaded, wiping at the tears that had escaped to slide down her cheek.

Mya nodded and looked aghast that she'd brought Iris to tears. "I'm sorry. I didn't mean to ruin your lunch," she said, on the verge of tears herself. "I just wanted to tell you…I wanted you to know…I'm sorry," she finished in defeat, shaking her head in remorse. "I'm so sorry."

Iris heard so much in that simple statement. She nodded and gave Mya's hand a squeeze. "You didn't ruin my lunch," she assured Mya, putting a brave smile on for her friend's benefit. "I'm fine. See? It was just a rough patch but give me a minute and I'll get through it."

Mya nodded but the sadness remained in her eyes. "I wish—"

Iris shushed her with a shake of her head. "None of that. If you're going to wish, wish for something useful like an influx of competent staff, new supplies or relocation out of the flood plain. Don't waste your wishes on something impossible."

Iris couldn't afford to play the wish game—the stakes were too high.

Chapter 9

Sierra, humming to herself to shake the odd feeling that she was being watched, hurried to her beat-up car and slipped inside, slamming the door with probably more force than was necessary. Safely locked inside, she released a shaky breath and laughed at her own jitters.

It was night but hardly late. Her father would skin her alive if she stayed out past ten o'clock on a school night but she'd taken the night shift at the general store to pick up a few extra bucks since she wasn't earning much working at the Tribal Center and she had a goal to reach.

Unlike her boyfriend, Vince, who had blown off work tonight to go to a party out at the run-down shack that belonged to one of their friends. He was supposed to be here with her so she wouldn't have to work the night shift alone. So much for chivalry. When she saw him tomorrow she'd make sure he knew how pissed she was when he tried to honey up to her at school.

Well, if Vince wanted to hang around on the rez for the rest of his life that was his malfunction. She had bigger dreams.

She planned on getting off the reservation and going to college someplace warm and beachy. Her dad thought she was going to attend Washington State but she'd been applying to colleges on the west coast of California. She wanted to go where the weather was mild and no one had reason to wear thermals or carry umbrellas at all times. She figured she'd break the news to her father as soon as she received an acceptance letter. Until then, it was all just hypothetical. In the meantime, she was saving every dime she could scrape up for that purpose.

That meant taking the occasional night shift at the general store.

She wasn't a jumpy girl but she'd had the distinct feeling that someone had been watching her as she'd walked to her car. The darkened treeline had never bothered her before, but suddenly it occurred to her that anyone could be hiding behind that forest curtain and that freaked her out more than a little.

Of course she was being silly, she rationalized as she turned the key in the ignition. The reservation was a safe place, filled with people she'd known her entire life.

She went to grab her purse to fish out her cell phone so she could call her dad—he always insisted she call when she worked late—and she jumped as something sharp jabbed her in the arm.

"Ow!" Sierra jerked and cried out just as an arm snaked around her neck from behind in the backseat and tightened until she could barely breathe. *Oh, God.*

"Please don't hurt me," she gasped, clutching at the arm cutting off her airway. "Please…"

"Shhh," her attacker crooned in her ear, even nuzzling her temple as if he were inhaling her scent and getting off on it. She tried to remember everything she'd ever learned in health class about self-defense techniques but fear had blotted out rational thought and she was left to struggle in half-blind panic as a strange lethargy started to seep into her muscles.

"Why…?" she asked, tears springing to her eyes.

The soft touch of lips against her temple seemed far more threatening than the cruel press of her attacker's forearm against her windpipe and she tried harder to get free but her head had begun to spin, leaving mush of her brain in its wake. She'd been drugged. She choked on bile as she gave one last flailing effort against her attacker.

When she could no longer struggle, and her hands had flopped uselessly to her sides as she slumped forward, she heard the door open and close, then open again. Cold air crept inside the cab of her car and she was lifted out and slung over her attacker's shoulder. She prayed for someone to come along but she knew it was a long shot. The store had closed an hour ago and everyone on the reservation knew it.

Her car, the little sedan her dad had scrimped and saved to give to her for her sixteenth birthday got farther and farther away as she was carried into the forest, away from the dim, flickering light of the parking lot, away from any semblance of safety or rescue.

From a far-off place in her mind, she thought of her dad and how he would grieve for her if she ended up dead. She'd promised him that she'd be careful but she often forgot to lock her car, especially when she ran late for work. Like tonight. *Daddy, I'm sorry...*

A swirling vortex of nothingness started to suck her down even as she fought it. Her limbs felt heavy and she was unable to lift her head or open her mouth to scream.

As she slipped from consciousness, she understood what her English teacher had been trying to teach about irony earlier that day in school.

She'd been worried about who might be in the forest... she should've been worried about who was in her car.

How ironic.

The following morning broke dismal and gray but having grown up in an area where sunshine was a treat and not the norm, Iris hardly noticed the inconvenience of a little drizzle. One thing she did notice, though, as she walked through the double doors of the clinic was Mya's pale and drawn face.

Her coffee thermos halfway to her lips, she paused when she saw Mya. "That's not a good sign," Iris murmured. "What's wrong?"

"I didn't want you to hear but I knew you'd find out this morning so I wanted to be the one to tell you. Sierra Buck was brought in last night," Mya said, wasting no time on preamble. "She was assaulted last night."

Iris swallowed but couldn't quite get the clot of fear and guilt to go down. Sierra? She was a kid. Barely sixteen if she remembered right. "What happened? And why didn't you call me last night?"

"I didn't want to upset you. It was too much to handle so soon after your own ordeal," Mya explained with quiet efficiency that spoke volumes. Like Iris, Mya had known Sierra since she was born. The girl had come into the clinic for her various cuts and bruises from early childhood, as well as her vaccinations and flu shots. And now she'd been attacked? Terrible guilt crashed down around Iris, battering her with the realization that someone else had been hurt because she'd stuck her head in the sand for her own protection. She gulped down the lump of grief and anguish with difficulty as Mya continued, "The night physician's assistant called me in and I handled the trauma."

"You should've called me," Iris said, her voice thin and reedy. She cleared her throat, trying to stay focused even though she felt as if she were sinking in quicksand. "I'm your lead nurse. I should've been here for you."

Mya waved away her protest and Iris let it go. There were certainly bigger issues at hand than her hurt feelings for being bypassed in the chain of command. Besides, she understood Mya was trying to protect her, even if Iris didn't want her coddling her like a damn baby. "Bastard left her in the woods. She could've caught pneumonia or been eaten by animals," Mya said, her bitterness escaping in her tone. "How could someone do this horrible thing? She's practically a child."

"A monster," Iris bit out. "A sick monster who doesn't care about anyone but himself." Rage had begun a slow percolation in her breast when she thought of Sierra victimized in this way. The rage smothered the guilt for the moment. "Where's Sierra now?" she asked.

"She's in room 1. I talked her dad into letting us keep her for observation. She's a mess emotionally. She hasn't said a word since she was brought in. I've called in a pysch evaluation for her but the psychiatrist on call is coming from two towns over. It'll be a while. In the meantime, we're just trying to keep her comfortable."

Iris nodded and wrapped her arms around herself,

feeling the warmth leaching from her body. "Did he...?"

Mya nodded, looking away. "And more."

"How bad?"

"She didn't require surgery to repair the damage but nearly so. She's pretty torn up." Mya's mouth tightened as she continued, "Sierra hadn't been sexually active yet. She was saving herself for marriage. There were vaginal lacerations as well as...in other places. Oh, Iris...my heart breaks for that girl."

"Great Spirit," Iris breathed, tears springing to her eyes. She ground out the moisture with the flat of her palm, angry that she felt so helpless. "Did you catch anything viable on the wet mount?" she asked, hoping Sierra's attacker hadn't had the wherewithal to use a condom, leaving behind essential forensic evidence.

"No DNA under her fingernails but since he drugs them into submission, that's not surprising and he must be wearing a condom when he rapes his victims," Mya answered, shaking her head. "The bastard is smart. He likely also wears gloves or something to keep from leaving fingerprints."

Iris stared, hardly able to say the words. "You think the two cases are related?" It was a stupid question. These kinds of crimes didn't happen often on the reservation, at least not on theirs. When Iris didn't answer, just met Mya's gaze, she shuddered. "Can I see her?"

Mya hesitated then relented. "Only for a few minutes. Sundance will be here soon to take her statement because last night she wasn't talking and she's not really up to visitors."

Iris walked to room 1 and before entering made sure she'd controlled her own heart rate first. She needed to be calm for Sierra. When she was ready, she opened the door and stepped inside. Sierra's father, James Buck, sat lightly dozing in a hard plastic chair beside Sierra's bedside. He jumped awake when Iris approached but settled when his gaze registered recognition.

"How is she?" Iris asked, checking Sierra's blood pressure and pulse. James's expression crumpled into such agony that she could almost feel his pain. Iris remained steadfast on the outside but inside she trembled. "Has she said anything?" she asked.

"When they first brought her in, she was so out of it, like she was on drugs or something," James stated, his gaze never leaving his daughter's face. "And then when the doc had managed to flush out whatever that monster had given her, she just stared at the wall not saying nothing." He looked to Iris, distraught. "You know my Sierra. She's a little butterfly. Always smiling, always saying something nice to everyone. Who would do this to her? Why?"

Iris shook her head, wishing she had the answer, not only for Sierra but for herself. Sierra appeared catatonic, rarely blinking, just staring at the wall as if her spirit had left behind the shell of her body. "Sierra?" Iris ventured, watching for any sign of life in the girl's brown eyes. Nothing, not even a flicker. She tried again, this time a little firmer. "Sierra, honey, it's me, Iris. Can you look at me?"

Again nothing and the failure to elicit a response only served to distress James further so Iris stopped. Perhaps in a few days Sierra would come around, Iris hoped.

"I didn't want her working the night shift," James started spontaneously, his eyes red-rimmed from a long night. "But she's trying to save up money to leave for college and there's so little work around here. She promised me she'd be safe."

A lump rose in Iris's throat as she nodded wordlessly. James had raised Sierra by himself after his girlfriend had split when Sierra had been only a year old. James could've gone the easy route and become a drunk like so many others before him who were faced with not enough work and too much vice, but he'd made being Sierra's dad his number one job. And now he was crumbling right before Iris's eyes over something no one had any control over.

"He dragged her into the woods and left her there like trash," James said, his voice trembling. "He hurt her so bad. She'll never be the same. He broke my little girl."

Iris couldn't get her mouth to work properly. She wanted to assure him that Sierra would recover eventually with plenty of love from her family and friends but she couldn't get herself to utter the words. She couldn't bear to give the man false hope. Besides, who was she to give advice on healing a wound like this? She was nowhere near better. Maybe on the surface she seemed put back together, but on the inside she was a shattered mess. Mya had been right not to call her, she realized as hot shameful tears crowded her eyes. She was certainly no help to this poor child. She was no help to anyone. She mumbled something appropriately apologetic to James and left the room before she embarrassed herself further and completely lost it.

Chapter 10

Sundance rounded the corner and Iris, head down and not watching where she was going, slammed into him, nearly knocking the wind out of him. She let out a small cry and instinctually struck at the solid wall that was his chest until she realized it was him.

"S-Sundance, I'm sorry," she said, moving to go around him but he stopped her with a gentle hand on her forearm. He tried not to take it personally when she flinched involuntarily at his touch but it served to kindle the cold rage he felt against the man preying on women.

"Are you okay?" he asked, wincing at the sore spot forming on his chest. She jerked a nod but her splotched face said otherwise. He took a guess that Mya had told her about Sierra. He knew it was going to be hard on Iris but he hadn't expected the wrench in his gut at her obvious struggle. "I take it you heard about Sierra?" At Iris's nod, he asked again, "Are you all right?"

"No, I'm not all right," Iris answered, a small, angry snap to her tone, but he sensed her response was more directed at herself than him. Iris had always been a proud woman, strong and opinionated. The subtle shake in her fingertips betrayed her innate fear of what she couldn't control. The change over her had been profound and he suspected she hated it but couldn't seem to stop it. It was as pointless as railing at the clouds for soaking the ground beneath them with a torrent of rainfall that overflowed the riverbank and flooded homes. She wiped her cheeks and rubbed the moisture on her blue scrub. "She was just a kid. A sweet, innocent kid on the brink of her life, getting ready to do great things. She had college plans and she couldn't wait to—" Her words seemed caught in her throat and she looked ready to collapse, which was the last thing she'd want anyone to see at work. "It's my fault," she cried, looking as if she wanted to sink into a dark hole and die. "I should've listened to you and tried harder to find out who did this but I was afraid and I didn't want to know. Now, that poor baby has to deal with what I'm going through and if it's nearly killing me, what's it going to do to that sweet girl? I can't bear to think of the damage…"

He pulled her into the empty staff lounge and closed the door before folding her into his arms. He did it without thought, and after a moment, she sagged against him. The scent of her long, black hair filled his senses as it trailed down her back from her no-nonsense ponytail and tickled the backs of his hands. He held her to him, willing some of his strength into her for what she was going through. She fitted perfectly against him, nestling into his chest like a puzzle piece clicking into place. The realization that he didn't want to let her go snapped him to attention. Her soft cries wet the front of his uniform but he didn't care. What mattered was getting Iris through this moment. Everything else would find its place later.

"You couldn't have known," he murmured, soothing her.

"It doesn't matter. He has to be stopped and you knew that but I shut you down. I couldn't handle it. This is my fault. For the rest of my life I'll know in my heart that Sierra was hurt because of me."

"Stop," he demanded, holding her tighter, but she didn't complain. In fact, she burrowed in harder, as if needing the pressure to reassure her that she was safe. He could feel her soft hiccups and erratic breathing against his chest. "You did not cause this. It happened because some sick freak gets his jollies off by hurting women. Plain and simple. I won't listen to you beat yourself up like this. You need to be strong. That's how you'll help Sierra. She needs your strength, to be an example of how you can pick yourself up and stand tall even when you've been knocked down."

She glanced up at him, her wet lashes framing eyes that conveyed fear and uncertainty. "What if I can't? I'm a mess. I'm the furthest thing from strong. Sierra needs a better example than me."

He didn't know how to tell her that he was in awe of her strength, her determination. That most people wouldn't have the courage to stare their situation in the face and march forward even when they were scared. But she did. She just couldn't see that in herself yet. His tongue felt tied and he wished for once he'd been born with the ability to say pretty things that inspired people. He felt inspired each time he looked at Iris but he couldn't seem to say that either without tripping over himself and looking like a fool, so he remained silent. All he could do was hold her. And so that's what he did.

After a long moment, Iris pulled away and almost couldn't meet his eyes. He handed her a tissue, that she gratefully accepted and wiped at her running nose. She inhaled a deep breath and managed a watery smile. "Not my finest moment." A faint, rueful smile followed. "I seem to be having a lot of those lately," she admitted. "I feel like such a toad. Sierra needs me to be strong, and here I am locked in the staff lounge bawling my eyes out. But I can't seem to control when and where the tears start."

"You've been through a lot," he said gruffly. "Don't beat yourself up for not being a superwoman."

"I'm not trying to be a superwoman," she said. "I just want to be *me* again."

"You will."

Silence laden with heartache filled the space between them until she offered quietly, "Thank you."

"You don't have to thank me," he said, though his body warmed and his arms itched to pull her close again. He shook off the thought with effort, needing to clear his head. A muddled brain was the last thing he needed, particularly when the stakes had just gotten higher. Someone was out there preying on the tribe's women. "I'd like you to rethink your decision to undergo hypnosis. Now that this man has struck twice, it's likely he won't stop until someone stops him. He thinks he's gotten away with his crimes but I aim to put him down. I can't do that without your help."

Iris shuddered but her mouth firmed. He caught a glimpse of the old Iris, the one who never backed down from a challenge and enjoyed the thrill of the chase as well as a bloody victory. She never apologized for being better or stronger and she was without a doubt, the best person to have as an advocate. He could see Iris shouldering that role with Sierra, no matter her own battle wounds. At that moment, pride suffused his body as he watched Iris grab on to the thinnest straw of courage she had within herself to face the demon in her nightmares for the sake of a young girl.

"I can't let this monster hurt anyone else if I can help it," Iris said. "Give me the name and number of this hypnotherapist. If the details in my head will catch this son of a bitch, I'll do it."

Sundance accepted her decision with a grave nod, knowing at what cost she had reached it. The moment wasn't appropriate to touch her but he wanted to. His heart swelled with something more than pride and he was caught between needing to push it away out of confusion and grabbing it with both hands to examine it. In the end, he thought it best to leave it be.

"If you're okay, I'm going to check and see if Sierra is ready to give a statement, though from what Mya has told me I don't have high hopes." She nodded and he opened the door but paused before leaving, needing to say one more thing before the moment was gone. Iris stood like a warrior, her eyes twin coals, not missing a single detail. She exuded beauty in spite of her wounds and he was momentarily stunned. He recovered without giving away the riot happening in his head. "You're a brave woman. I never knew just how brave until this moment. I won't let you down."

Her lips parted as if to say something but he didn't wait to listen. He didn't dare. His thoughts were already a twisted mess and he needed clarity, not confusion.

But he couldn't deny, somewhere along the way, he'd stopped seeing Iris as the friend of his sister that he tolerated and more like the woman she'd turned into when he hadn't been paying attention.

If only he'd come to this realization before that night…maybe she wouldn't have been in that bar that night.

Too bad *maybe* didn't mean squat.

The monster was still out there—and there was no telling who he was going to target next.

Sundance left Iris and went straight to Sierra's room. He knocked softly and entered, steeling himself for the sight of young Sierra Buck in much the same state he'd seen her when she'd been found.

He accepted a handshake from James Buck and knew without having to ask that not much had changed. He withheld a sigh, not wanting to further distress James. He could only imagine what the man was going through, and Sundance wasn't going to add to his burden.

"How are you holding up?" he asked James.

James shook his head. "Not good. I'm trying to hold it together but it's hard."

"I'm going to do my best to find who did this," he promised James.

James nodded but refrained from comment. What was there to say? Not much. Sundance sighed and took out his notepad. "I hate to do this but I have to ask some questions." When James nodded his consent, Sundance continued. "How long had Sierra been working the late shift at the general store? Was this something she did often?"

"Not too often but no one wanted to work the late shift, which made it an easy shift to pick up for extra cash. She was saving money for college. I didn't like her working at night but she assured me it was safe."

"What about her coworkers? Who did she close with? Isn't there supposed to be two people closing the store?"

"I thought Vince—that's her boyfriend—was supposed to close with her but he blew off work to go to some party. I could skin that boy alive for leaving her all alone like that," James spat but his ire soon faded and he just looked sad and bereft. "It ain't the boy's fault. He's feeling pretty bad about it. I just want someone to blame, I guess."

"I understand. I'll want to talk to the boy. Where can I find him?"

"He's at home today on account of the situation. He's the one who found Sierra. He'd come back to pick up his car and found Sierra lying in the dirt like she'd crawled out of the forest and then passed out there."

That's quite likely what happened. The drug—ketamine if the rapist used the same MO—had worn off enough to shake off the paralysis but had still been potent enough to keep her from walking far. According to Mya, the girl had been naked and beaten in addition to sexually assaulted. It was a miracle she'd found her senses long enough to crawl out of the forest. As dense as the undergrowth was in that area, no one would've seen her even from the parking lot. The rapist had obviously known this, that was why he'd picked that particular area. That told Sundance the rapist was at the very least familiar with the landscape.

Sundance had a bad feeling that whoever this sick freak was…he was no stranger.

He might even be one of the tribe.

Chapter 11

Sundance walked into the Tribal Center with his documentation tucked under his arm. He saw Chad through the glass talking with a stout, older man he recognized as his father, the director of Indian affairs. Chad's expression was thunderous—an expression he didn't often see—but over the years he'd gotten the impression that Chad and his father didn't get along. If he was always trying to cut Chad's funding wherever he went, Sundance could see how that might strain the relationship.

He knocked and Chad ushered him in with a tight smile. "There's the man of the hour," he announced, gesturing. "I was just telling my father of all the uses a tribal officer offers to a reservation and why it would be shortsighted to make cuts at this time."

Sundance stuck his hand out, grinding his jaw against

the urge to start throwing numbers and stats at the man. "Sundance Jonson, tribal officer," he said.

"Paul Brown. I remember you. Last time I saw you, you were a bit shorter," he said, taking his seat opposite Sundance.

Sundance exchanged a mildly amused look with Chad. "Yes, sir, I've grown a little since I was twelve." Paul patted his rounded belly. "Haven't we all…" Then he got straight to business. "I hear there's been a bit of a situation happening here with some assaults against women?"

Reluctant to use the assaults as a platform but knowing it would probably have the most impact he moved forward with a nod. "We seem to have someone targeting women on the reservation. The last victim was a high school student who worked in this very office in the work experience program."

"I told you about Sierra Buck," Chad reminded his father. "Remember? I told you I hired her using grant funds."

Paul paused for a moment, his stare narrowing in thought then his mouth cracked into a smile, which Sundance found inappropriate given the situation. "That's right. Sweet girl. I met her when she was going through the interview process. What a shame she was hurt. The office ought to expense some flowers for the girl."

Sundance looked to Chad in confusion, prompting Chad to explain quickly. "The day my father decided to make his first stop to check in on me, I was interviewing students for the position. It was a very brief meeting, I'm surprised he remembered her at all."

Paul chuckled. "I always remember a pretty face. Now—" he lost his mirth and returned to being the bear of his reputation "—tell me why, aside from this newest information, why your position is justified when the whole of the actual reservation is only one square mile. There are bigger reservations than yours with less resources. Why should yours receive more than their share?"

Sundance fought the desire to snap in the face of such an attitude but he managed to keep his cool. "As you're probably aware, we have a proposal in the works to increase the tribe's land to include portions of the Olympic National Forest. When that happens, we'll need more than one more tribal officer," he explained with the patience due a saint. Sundance put the stats he'd worked on all night to produce in Paul's hand. "This shows you what I'm dealing with—not counting the assaults, which are taking all my time, so any poaching, land use violations, or less violent crimes are taking a backseat, and trust me, it shows. The call volume has increased for petty crime. Poor Cece is working double time answering the phone. Another officer could also be used to relieve our dispatcher."

Sundance spent the next hour reminding Paul Brown why the tribe was unique and why cutting the tribal officer would be like giving chaos free rein. By the time Paul left, Sundance felt he'd given it his best shot, though to be truthful, he didn't like Paul one bit. He saw a man who smiled with his mouth but not his eyes and he didn't trust that quality in a man.

After Paul had taken his leave, Chad seemed happy to be rid of him.

"Typical bureaucrat, huh?" he said to Sundance. "But I think you made some good points, better than I could've. My father appreciates a straight answer and you gave him that at least."

"I'd have thought your dad would be more sympathetic to our cause having lived here for a time," Sundance said.

"Well, we weren't here long. We moved here when I was five and only stayed until I was twelve. And he's not Hoh either. This place was just a job for him on his way up the BIA ladder. Sorry, but if it means anything, this place was special to me and I agree with everything you told him."

Sundance nodded and he was glad the meeting went well but his mind kept snagging on Paul's reaction to Sierra's assault. It was as if his interest in the girl had been purely because she'd been pretty. The offer to send flowers had been cursory. "Does your father plan to visit often?" he asked.

Chad shrugged. "Hope not, but who knows. Sometimes he takes a special interest in the tribes he oversees. There's no rhyme or reason to it, either, so it's hard to predict. My hope is that there isn't enough to keep him interested." He nudged Sundance with a wink. "We'd better keep him away from that pretty sister of yours, right?" Sundance narrowed his stare, not liking the idea of Paul Brown anywhere near his sister. Chad sobered, realizing the joke had been in bad taste. "Sorry. Don't worry, I got your back. Besides, my dad only likes girls who aren't a challenge. I'm pretty sure Mya would tell him—nicely, of course—that she wasn't interested."

"So your father is still single?" he asked, trying to gain some kind of insight into the man. He didn't remember Chad's mother being around back in the day.

"Ever since *Mamacita* left back when I was in diapers, Dad hasn't bothered to remarry. Just me and the old man. Dad used to joke that she never left, she was just buried in the backyard." Chad laughed as if that were actually funny. An odd chill slithered down Sundance's back. Chad's laugh ended on a sigh. "My dad always had an odd sense of humor. Anyway, I hate to cut and run but I promised I'd meet the old man at The Dam Beaver for a lunchtime cocktail. Now having reacquainted yourself with him, you can probably understand why in his previous career he worked exclusively with animals."

"What do you mean? I don't remember that," Sundance said.

"Well, before he went into government work, he was a veterinarian. After we left here, he started a side business out of our home, mostly for weekend calls. That way, it didn't interfere with the day job. I know, it's a weird thing to have as a side thing but that's my dad. He doesn't care what it looks like."

"If he likes animals so much, why didn't he just stick with his veterinary practice?"

"Not enough money, I guess. Besides, he's mostly just on call in case the local vet needs someone in a pinch. It's not like he's actually running a practice again."

Sundance nodded as if he understood, but it all sounded pretty strange to him. To each his own, he supposed.

However, he didn't like the idea of Paul Brown spending too much time on the reservation. Somehow, that man set off bells in Sundance's head and when that happened, he listened.

Iris saw a man carrying flowers walking with the intent to enter Sierra's room and she hustled over to block him. "Who are you?"

Her reaction surprised him but he recovered quickly

with a disarming smile. "Brutally straightforward, I see," he said, chuckling as if amused by her manner, which only served to annoy her further. When her expression neither lightened nor improved, he gave up the attempts to charm her and simply said, "Chad Brown, Indian Affairs liaison. I've only been around for a few weeks but I used to live here when I was a kid, until I was about twelve. My father is the Director of Indian Affairs. I'm the tribal liaison for the time being until my father decides to move me again."

"You move around a lot?" she asked.

"More so than I'd like. But actually, I'm considering making this my permanent post. I always liked it here. The people are solid and I like to fish."

She didn't know what to think of this Chad Brown but he seemed harmless enough. In her previous life, she would've been flirting shamelessly with the good-looking stranger but now she saw the boogeyman in every shadow and she trusted no one, least of all a handsome outsider.

But she grudgingly realized that she may be overreacting a touch and let up the pressure incrementally. "The flowers are beautiful. I'm sure Sierra will appreciate them."

Chad smiled and started to walk away. "Nice to meet you…?"

He was fishing for her name.

"Nurse Beaudoin," she said, not interested in sharing.

"You're a beautiful woman, Nurse Beaudoin," Chad said, not the least bit put off by her disinterest. If anything, he seemed tickled by it.

She should've been flattered, but instead, she felt vulnerable. Perhaps she shouldn't have worn her hair down. Hating the fact that she automatically sought blame for his attention, she stiffened and shot Chad a cool smile saying, "Good day, Mr. Brown," before walking away to find a vase for the flowers. She didn't pause in her stride, nor did she check to see if he had indeed left as she hoped but she did note as she entered the staff lounge that her hands were shaking.

Mya found her as she was filling the vase with water and exclaimed when she saw the flowers. "Wow, who's the lucky girl?"

Iris's smile was brief as she said, "They're for Sierra. Her boss bought them."

"Duke bought Sierra flowers?" Mya asked, no doubt trying to reconcile the image of the tattooed and grizzled manager of the general store, who wasn't really known for his people skills, even walking into a florist shop.

"Not Duke. A man named Chad Brown. Apparently, he's the new Indian liaison over at the Tribal Center? He said he used to live here. Do you know him?"

"Oh, that's right. Sundance told me about him. I don't remember him but he was friends with Sundance. Apparently, they kept in touch over the years. How sweet of him to think of Sierra," Mya said.

Iris finished rearranging the flowers and prepared to take them to Sierra. "Well, I thought it was weird. And I think he's weird."

"Really?" Mya said, frowning. "Why?"

Iris shrugged. "I don't know," she admitted, suddenly feeling flustered by her reaction. She had no reason to feel awkward or hesitant around the new guy, which led her to conclude that she was overreacting because of her experience. Tears pricked her eyes but she blinked them back, refusing to let them fall. "It's nothing. I'm sure he's fine. It just took me by surprise, is all."

Mya understood, saying, "It'll get better. You'll find your footing again. It just takes time."

Iris nodded but she didn't share Mya's confidence. Inside, she felt as though everything was wrong, tipped upside down and backward. What she'd known seemed suspect and what she didn't know terrified her. And now Sierra was on the same horrifying ride. Her fingers tightened around the vase and she had to consciously loosen them before she cracked the glass. She forced a smile and moved toward the door, saying to Mya, "Of course. Time heals all wounds, right?"

"Well, that is the saying but even though it's a cliché, there's some truth to it," Mya said.

Iris smiled, though she knew it didn't reach her eyes as she said, "We'll see." But she didn't believe there would ever be enough time to heal what had been broken inside of her.

A few days later Sundance returned to the Tribal Center and went straight to Chad's office but not before giving the grant guy a solid stare on the way in. He'd had to handle some other cases before returning to the assaults but the days between had made him antsy, feeling as if every minute that ticked by was taking him further away from catching the person responsible.

"Listen, I'm doing some legwork on Sierra Buck's case and I need to know everyone who had contact with Sierra here at the center."

"Okay," Chad agreed, but his face was marred by a slight frown. "But why here? She wasn't attacked here…surely you don't think someone at the center was responsible for this?"

Sundance let his gaze rest on Brett through the glass of Chad's office. "Just following all leads."

"Come on, now. You're eyeing my grant guy as if he's a suspect, which I'm sure he's not. He's a good guy. Married and everything."

"Just because he's married doesn't mean squat. People, particularly sociopaths, live double lives all the time. It's part of the thrill."

Chad followed his stare and seemed contemplative. "I hate to think of anyone in my office capable of something so brutal but I guess you're right. This is why you're the investigator and I push paper all day," he said with self-deprecating good humor. "Whatever you need, just name it."

Satisfied, Sundance said, "I want to talk with your grant man. He seemed pretty chatty with Sierra the other day and it rubbed me wrong."

"Of course," Chad said. "Just try to remember, there's no law against being friendly and try not to scare him away. We need him." Chad caught Brett's eye and gestured him inside. "Listen, I'll let you two talk here in my office while I run a few errands," he offered, sliding on his coat.

Sundance thanked Chad and stepped aside as a very nervous-looking man walked in.

Chad clapped Brett on the shoulder in a friendly gesture but his expression remained serious, which Sundance appreciated. "This is the tribal officer, Sundance Jonson. He wants to talk to you regarding Sierra Buck. I've told him our office will do whatever is needed to help bring Sierra's attacker to justice." Chad nodded to Sundance before heading out the door.

Brett smiled and seemed to loosen up but there remained a wariness about him that instantly put Sundance on alert.

"How well do you know Sierra Buck?" he asked.

"She's the intern. I know her as well as anyone else here in the office."

"The other day you seemed pretty chatty with her, flirtatious even. I heard you're married…"

"Nothing wrong with talking with someone," Brett said. "No law against it as far as I know."

"Do you always flirt with underage girls?" he asked.

Brett's mouth tightened mulishly. "No, of course not."

"So you made an exception for Sierra? Understandable. She's a very pretty girl," Sundance said. "Where were you last night between the hours of 11:00 p.m. and 1:00 a.m.?"

"Asleep. With my wife at home."

"Will your wife corroborate that claim?"

"Of course she will because it's true."

Sundance made a few notes. "I'll need your wife's number so I can verify your whereabouts."

Brett rattled off a number. "Anything else?"

"You don't seem very upset about Sierra."

He had the grace to flush. "Of course I am. I was shocked when I heard."

Sundance took a moment to gauge Brett's reaction. He sensed nervousness. It could be nothing. Or it could be he had something to hide. Closing his notebook, he gestured to the door. "I'll be in touch. You can go."

Brett wasted little time in escaping to his desk and Sundance let himself out. He'd follow up with the wife when he returned to the station. He was tempted to drop by the clinic and check on Iris but he couldn't find a suitable reason to do so, so he didn't.

But it didn't stop his thoughts from circling around Iris, buzzing his brain with irritating frequency. Frankly, this was a complication he didn't need but that didn't seem to matter.

Sundance scrubbed his face with his palms and climbed into his Durango.

Focus... He'd sort his feelings out later when the sick freak responsible for the vicious assaults was behind bars...or dead.

Chapter 12

Sundance gripped the handle above his head as Iris hurtled down the highway, seemingly oblivious to her speed, the pouring rain and the fact that he felt ready to puke.

He'd never been carsick in his life until now.

Right at that moment he was rethinking his agreement to let her drive to the hypnotherapist's office. He'd been surprised when she'd called, asking if he'd go with her, but when he heard the slight tremor in her voice, he didn't hesitate.

"Iris, there is a speed limit," he reminded her from between clamped lips. "Let's try and get to our destination in one piece." Iris glanced at her speedometer and reluctantly eased up on the gas. Sundance didn't even try to hide his relief. "Thank you," he said, eliciting a small flustered smile from Iris.

"Sorry…my head is…well, not where it should be, I

guess." She shot him a quick look. "Thanks for agreeing to come with me. I was going to ask Mya but she's been having a hard time finding anyone to cover for her at the clinic and I feel bad enough as it is leaving her shorthanded so I could make this appointment."

He understood. "It's not a problem. I appreciate you seeing Dr. Seryn. I know it won't be easy."

Iris nodded and swallowed, letting silence fill the space between them, no doubt her mind racing with all the fears and doubts that came with doing something like this.

"So tell me how you know this woman?" Iris asked, her tone betraying her nervousness. "I mean, is she reputable? Does she know what she's doing?"

"She's very reputable and, yes, she knows what she's doing. I wouldn't send you to an amateur."

"How'd you meet her?" Iris asked.

It was a fair question considering they were traveling off the reservation, outside of Forks to the woman's private studio. Still, the reason he knew of a hypnotherapist wasn't one he often shared. But since Iris was facing the unknown on his urging, he figured he owed her one. "She helped me get through some things," he said. "I started having nightmares. They came out of the blue, too. I figured they'd stop eventually but it got so bad I started to avoid sleeping and in my job, I can't let fatigue get in the way. When I fell asleep at my desk between calls, I knew I had to find a way to fix whatever was causing the nightmares."

"And you thought of hypnosis?" Iris asked.

"Not at first," he admitted. "I wasn't open to the idea when Mya first suggested it but she'd known this woman from med school who had gone into hypnotherapy as a side thing. After another week of night terrors, I was ready to throw in the towel. I made the appointment with Dr. Seryn." While sharing his vulnerabilities wasn't high on his list of desirable things to do, somehow focusing on anything other than Iris's driving made it easier to ease up on the handle and actually breathe. "It took a few sessions—and really, I didn't know if it was working or not—until one day I realized where my nightmares were coming from. Once that happened, I was able to sleep again."

"So where were your nightmares originating from?" she asked.

"A childhood incident that I'd forgotten about," he said, flashing to the memory. "One with my mother."

She fell silent and he knew she was remembering his mother, Betty. She'd been a troubled woman, most likely bipolar and self-medicating with alcohol, but the health care system back then wasn't the same as it was now and the help simply hadn't been there. He knew that now, but through the eyes of a kid Betty's unpredictable mood swings had been frightening.

"What happened?"

He didn't want to talk about it. The memories of his parents weren't filled with good times. They'd both fought their demons, and in the end, the demons had won. His parents had died in a drunk driving accident when he and Mya had been young. His grandparents had taken over the job, though in reality it'd been Sundance who had raised both himself and Mya because their grandparents had been too old to truly care for them. Theirs was a story not unlike many on the reservation. Iris knew this because her childhood had been similar in ways. "It wasn't a good memory, which is probably why I buried it."

"And she helped uncover it?"

"Yeah."

Iris nodded and fell into reflective silence again. Iris was a smart woman. He could guess that she was thinking of what Dr. Seryn might uncover of that night. He'd been so sure this was the right thing to do but he wasn't sure if he was prepared for the cost. Could Iris handle what was uncovered? He couldn't be certain but something told him that she could. If not for herself, then for Sierra.

They pulled into a leaf-strewn driveway and parked alongside an A-frame cottage. Iris unbuckled her seat belt and looked inquiringly at Sundance. "This is it? She works out of her home?"

"She has a studio out back," he answered, stepping out of the Bronco. "Like I said, this is a side job for her. Like a hobby, I guess."

"Odd hobby," Iris murmured, her nerves strung taut, but she followed Sundance as he headed toward the detached studio behind the home. She kept Sierra's face in her memory, reminding her that something bigger than herself was at stake because if she didn't, she would've returned to her Bronco and drove home like the wind.

They entered through a white-washed Dutch door into a comfortable studio apartment that spoke of relaxation and tranquility. A large fountain burbled in the corner, surrounded by lush potted plants of every variety, overly large, sumptuous throw pillows made from soft cotton lay on a plush chaise and mild strains of violin floated in from invisible speakers.

It was all perfectly lovely—and Iris wanted to bolt.

"Welcome." A cheery, smiling blonde looked up from her notebook as they walked in. She stood. "You must be Iris. Sundance has told me very nice things about you."

Iris's brow rose. What sort of things? She shot Sundance a quick look but she didn't have time for much else because the doctor had clasped Iris's hand in a tight but reassuring gesture as she introduced herself.

"I'm Dr. Emily Seryn, but you can certainly call me Emily if you prefer. Sometimes the whole doctor thing can be off-putting. Please, take a seat. Let's get acquainted."

"Pleased to meet you, Emily," Iris murmured, avoiding the chaise and taking a seat in the oversize chair. Sundance followed her lead and sat in the corresponding seat. She let her stare flit around the room in an attempt to find something else to talk about aside from what she was really there to talk about. But it didn't matter if she babbled on about the weather or the expensive art on the walls. Eventually they'd find their way to what the doctor was paid to do, so Iris drew a deep breath and jumped in. "How does this work?"

Emily smiled. "I appreciate your straightforward manner. That will work in your favor because you want to get to the root of things. Some people come here wanting to magically find the answers to their problems but aren't willing to do the hard work to find what they seek. I sense you're not that kind of person."

Iris accepted the praise. She prided herself on her work ethic and she supposed taking on this challenge was no different from anything else she'd undertaken in her life. She wouldn't back down, no matter how hard she was shaking. She looked to Sundance. "Do you stay during the session?" she asked.

Emily answered for him. "No. The sessions are private. Today's meeting is simply to get to know one another, so that you feel comfortable coming on your own."

"Oh." Iris felt the tension drain from her shoulders but she was oddly disappointed, too. "I guess that's a good idea," she conceded, admitting, "I was trying to psych myself up for whatever was going to happen today. False alarm." She gave a short, rueful laugh. "Is everyone this nervous their first time?"

Emily laughed, the sound easy and without judgment. "It depends. I think most people who've had no experience with hypnosis fear that somehow they're going to end up being persuaded to do something out of character like barking like a dog or squawking like a chicken the way they do in those Vegas shows but it's not really like that. When you get away from the stage entertainment, it's basically about altering your brain waves to achieve a hyperrelaxed state. Think of your brain as a giant computer capable of storing billions of bits of data, some of it stored in areas not readily accessed by your conscious mind. The power to do anything is tucked away in your mind, as are details you might've forgotten or buried." Iris swallowed. She feared the buried bits in her head. Emily continued, her voice steady and calm but with an undercurrent of compassion. "Sundance has told me of your ordeal. I've worked with victims of violent attacks and together we've achieved a satisfying level of success. I would like the opportunity to help you navigate what you're going through."

"I—I'm fine. I need help remembering so Sundance can catch whoever did this to me and another person, a teenage girl I've known since she was a baby."

"Yes, Sundance told me. And we'll do what we can

to unlock those blank spots in your mind. But I can help you with other aspects of your trauma, as well."

And allow someone to poke around in her head for longer than was necessary? No thanks. Iris smiled. "I appreciate your offer but I just want to find something useful for Sundance and then put all of this behind me."

"Very good then," Emily said, though her tone made Iris suspicious. It was as if she were agreeing only because she knew, in time, Iris would change her mind. Well, Emily seemed like a very nice woman but there was no way Iris was going to change her mind on that score.

They chatted a bit more, getting to know one another and by the time Iris and Sundance left, Iris felt more comfortable with the idea of coming on her own. She agreed to see Emily the following week.

"She's real nice," Iris said as they climbed into the Bronco to leave. "She has a way about her that's very... Zen-like. Does that sound weird?"

"No. That's Emily. She has a gift for relaxing people. Mya said in med school Emily was one of the only students the anatomy professor couldn't bully because she managed to turn him into jelly with her voice." Sundance broke out into a smile, his full mouth tilting in a way that made her notice how soft and sensitive his lips were. Iris looked away, discomfited with the train of her thoughts. "Are you okay?" he asked, noting her sudden change in mood.

"I'm fine."

"You say that a lot," he said. "But the more you say it, the less I believe it. Talk to me, Iris. I'll listen."

"Why?" she countered, mentally telling herself to shut up but her mouth wouldn't listen. "Why would you listen? Why are you being so…caring all of a sudden? Don't you recall that we don't like each other? We never have? I mean, I can remember plenty of times when we've both said some mean things to one another and I'm pretty sure neither one of us was sorry for it, either." Of course, she knew the answer but she wished it were something deeper, like Mya said. A frustrated well of sadness swamped her. "It's the case. You're all about the job. It's what you're good at and that's okay—"

"Iris—"

"No, really, I understand. I just wish…" She bit her lip in time before she blurted out what was really making her heart beat erratically, but she wished she had the guts to throw her feelings out there. "Oh, crap. Never mind." She took a corner too fast and the Bronco skidded a little on the wet asphalt. She hadn't lost control of the vehicle but it was enough to cause her to take notice of her speed and the fact that Sundance was white-knuckling the handle above his head.

"I'm sorry—"

"Pull over." It wasn't a polite request, it was a demand. "Now."

"Calm down," she groused, not about to take orders. It was her car. If he'd wanted to drive he should've offered to take his Durango. Oh, wait, he had. She shrugged off that last thought. "Stop being such a wuss. I've slowed down."

"You're driving like a maniac. Pull over before you kill us both."

She shot him an incredulous look, surprised when she saw how serious he was. *Unbelievable.* Even more unbelievable was that she was doing it. She pulled onto the gravel shoulder and let the Bronco idle in neutral. The rain, a steady drizzle, kept the wipers going at a continuous pace. "What now?" she asked, annoyed at him for being such a baby and herself for being so reckless. She supposed she had taken that corner too fast. Maybe he was right. Her hands were shaking again. She fisted her palms in an effort to will the quake away but it didn't work. Suddenly, his hands covered hers, causing her to jump slightly. Her knee-jerk reaction was to pull away but when she caught Sundance's stare she stilled.

"I didn't offer to listen because of the case," he said quietly. The sharp odor of wet soil and evergreen mingled with the scent she associated with Sundance. Together they created a spicy mix that made her yearn for the simplicity of the days before the attack. The old Iris might've leaned over and sampled those lips without reservation. Or maybe she might not have. She wasn't sure any longer. So, she remained paralyzed with his hands covering hers, wondering what to do. When he was sure he had her attention, he continued somberly, "I offered because I want to. You're right, we haven't always been civil to each other but things have changed."

"What's changed?" she whispered. "Because I was attacked? I don't want your pity, or anyone else's."

"I could never pity you. Pity is reserved for weaklings and cowards. You're neither of those things. You're a warrior, Iris. If nothing else, I respect that."

If nothing else… Tears stung her eyes. She wanted more than his respect but how could she hope for more when she had nothing to give in return? She withdrew her hands and gripped the steering wheel. He pulled away and she sensed a change. She couldn't blame him. She felt as frigid as a meat locker inside. "I apologize for driving so carelessly. I'll slow down, 'kay?"

He sighed and looked away. "I'd appreciate that. Living to see tomorrow is high on my list."

"Ha." She smirked, though it took effort. "Humor is good. When all else fails, if you haven't lost your ability to laugh, you still have a chance."

"A chance at what?"

"Hell if I know. I never understood that saying." She pulled onto the road and in an effort to avoid the awkward silence, she switched on the radio.

And for the rest of the ride, classic rock took the place of painful conversation.

Deep inside in her chest, something keened while another part of her seethed with rage over what had been taken from her and from every woman who'd ever had the power over her body ripped away by another.

She sent a silent prayer to Great Spirit for peace—and if not peace—vengeance.

Surely, that wasn't too much to ask?

Chapter 13

Sundance went over his notes on the rape cases, looking for clues he might've missed the first go around. He'd since talked with Brett Duncan's wife, who had, as expected, verified her husband's alibi. That brought him back to square one.

Iris and Sierra had been beaten, which suggested rage. There'd been no epithelials beneath either woman's fingernails when Mya had done the scrapings, and while the DNA analysis had yet to return from the Department of Justice labs, there'd been no sign of semen.

He sifted through his research on rapist profiles looking for anything that stood out in similarity. If rape was an act of control, the attacker sought to find control over something he ordinarily wouldn't have. Was the man a loner? Someone who couldn't get women? Perhaps someone who was awkward and socially backward? Sundance's instinct told him the attacker had been incensed that Iris had dared to fight back even after the dose of ketamine. Maybe that's why he'd given Sierra such a big dose of ketamine—he'd wanted to be sure Sierra couldn't lift a finger to stop him. But why had he brutalized the poor girl so badly? Perhaps he'd been irritated by something else, and he'd taken out his frustration on her helpless body. Who knows?

What were the similarities? Sundance searched for the answer. Both women were attractive, highly so. Both were spunky and charismatic. Almost larger than life. Perhaps the attacker harbored a deep fear of women, particularly women who seemed out of his league. Was it only Native American women?

Picking up the phone, he placed a call to the neighboring reservation where it went to voice mail. He left a message and tried another reservation. Washington State was dotted with tribal land and he didn't think he'd have much luck calling every tribal office in the hopes of stumbling on something, but he was at his wit's end by now and nearing desperation.

Each day that went by was a day that the attacker got away with his crime. And that curdled his stomach.

His cell phone went off and he saw that Mya was calling.

"What's up, sis?" he asked, checking off the last reservation he'd called, getting ready to move on to the next.

"I thought you might like to know that Sierra is no longer catatonic. She's talking. Did you want to take her statement?"

Hell yes, he did. "I'll be there in ten minutes."

True to his word, within ten minutes he was striding down the hall toward Sierra's room. He wasn't surprised to see Iris there by the teen's bedside. James stood by the window, his shoulders tense. Sundance suspected this would be very difficult for James to hear and his tension would only make it worse for Sierra.

"James, why don't you go take a walk outside for a bit," he suggested, to which James shook his head resolutely, no.

"It's okay, Dad," Sierra said, her voice small. "I'd rather you step outside, please. I don't want you to hear."

James looked stricken and ready to protest but he finally understood that Sundance's request had been a mercy for them both and jerked a short nod before saying, "You holler if you need me. I'll just be outside the door."

"Thanks, Dad."

Iris rose as if to leave but Sierra caught her hand. "Please stay," she pleaded, her big brown eyes wide pools of fear and vulnerability. Sierra turned to Sundance. "Is it okay if she stays?"

"Of course," he answered, feeling an all-over-body sadness for this young girl and what she was going through. It only served to push him harder. He swore privately he'd find who did this. But for the moment, he had to take her statement, no matter how difficult. He, for one, was glad Iris agreed to stay. He wasn't great with tears and he could tell Sierra's weren't far from the surface.

Iris patted Sierra's hand with reassurance. "You remember Sundance, right? He's the tribal officer and he's going to write down the events as you remember them."

"What if I don't remember a lot? Will you still be able to catch him?" she asked.

"I'll do my best," he promised.

Sierra nodded, looking to Iris for strength. She drew a deep breath as if bolstering herself and waited for Sundance to begin the questioning.

He flipped his notepad and with pen poised, said, "Sierra, tell me from the beginning what you remember."

"I closed that night. Vince was supposed to close with me but he blew me off for some party."

"How long have you and Vince dated?"

"Almost six months. He was the first guy willing to wait…" Tears welled in her eyes and Sundance looked to Iris for help. She wordlessly complied, handing Sierra a tissue with an understanding smile. Sierra accepted the tissue and wiped at her eyes and nose. "Anyway, so it was just me closing that night. The parking lot was empty and even though I told Duke only one streetlamp in the parking lot worked, he hadn't fixed the other two yet so it was pretty dark. But I always parked near the working streetlamp because my dad said it was safer. I got to my car and got in. The next thing I knew something sharp had poked me in the arm."

"We didn't find a syringe in the car but your arm did have a puncture wound," Sundance said. "Did you see who had injected you?"

Sierra shook her head. "He was behind me. He'd put his arm around my throat and held me against the h-headrest. He had a funny smell, like balloons." She choked on the memory, her voice going choppy and tight. "H-he smelled my hair and k-kissed my temple. I tried to remember what I'd been taught in my self-defense class but my mind went blank. I was so scared."

Iris murmured soothing words to calm Sierra who'd begun to sob into her hands. He waited until Iris had managed to stem the tide of tears. Sierra blew her nose and apologized but Sundance said, "No apologies are needed, sweetheart. If you need to cry, go ahead." She nodded and Iris squeezed her hand in encouragement. "Take all the time you need," he said.

Sierra wiped her nose before continuing. "The drug worked pretty fast. Within minutes I couldn't move my arms and legs. He dragged me out of the car and slung me over his shoulder. The last thing I saw was my car and the forest floor."

Sierra looked utterly defeated that she had so little by the way of details to share, and another tear slipped down her cheek. Iris wiped it away, saying gently, "This wasn't your fault. You're doing the best that you can and that's good enough."

Sundance pictured the scene in his head. Frowning, he said, "Sierra…did you see his shoes?"

Sierra searched her memory while wiping her nose. After a moment, she answered slowly, as if retrieving the detail with difficulty. "Yeah, he wore fancy ones, like something you'd wear to an office," she said. "Does that mean something?"

"It all means something," he assured the teen, sharing a look with Iris, wondering if she was thinking what he was thinking. When he and Mya had cataloged Iris's wounds and bruises, they'd taken a photograph of a bruise likely caused by a shoe on her thigh. There hadn't been any ridges in the shoe impression, which meant it hadn't been a hiking boot or a tennis shoe. He'd suspected a dress shoe. The fact that Sierra remembered the dress shoes specifically sealed his theory that the two attacks were related. He returned to Sierra. "Do you remember anything else? Did he wear cologne? Did his breath smell like anything in particular?"

Sierra shook her head. "Not that I remember. Just the

balloon smell. I think it was from his gloves but I'm not sure. I'm sorry."

Iris rubbed her arm. "Hey, remember? No sorries. You're doing great."

"Yes, you are," Sundance agreed. "Now tell me what you remember next."

"It's fuzzy. I was hurting all over. I was cold. It was almost morning. Somehow I dragged myself out of the woods and back to the parking lot. I guess Vince found me and brought me to the urgent care clinic."

"How did Vince know to look for you at the store?"

"I was supposed to meet him at the party after work. I told my dad I was going to stay at a friend's house so he wasn't expecting me at home. When I didn't show up at the party, he came looking for me."

"Sounds like a good guy," Sundance said.

"Yeah," Sierra agreed, giving a little watery sniff. "He feels pretty bad. He thinks this is his fault for leaving me alone."

"Well, that's natural. He probably feels like he should've been protecting you when you got hurt."

"I tried to tell him it's not his fault."

Sundance smiled. He knew how the kid felt. Somehow he felt he should've been able to prevent what had happened to Iris, though how he wasn't sure. Feelings weren't rational, that was for sure. "He can be there for you now. That's what's important, okay?"

She nodded. Before Sundance could ask any more questions, James poked his head in, visibly worried about his daughter and Sundance didn't blame him. The kid had been through hell. Sundance waved James in. "Go ahead and come in. We're done. Sierra did great. She helped me a lot."

James nodded but it seemed he had aged ten years since Sierra's attack. He handed James a business card with his phone numbers on it. "If she remembers anything else, just call my cell. Day or night." A tight-lipped nod followed but Sundance knew James would make the call if needed. He advised Sierra with mock sternness, "Rest up so you can get out of here and back to your own bed. I know I never sleep well unless it's in my own bed."

Sierra smiled but it didn't reach her eyes and that killed him. So young and now burdened with such pain. It wasn't fair.

He let himself out and within minutes Iris was behind him. "Wait up," she called out, causing him to stop and turn. Unexpected warmth shone in her eyes as she said, "You were really good with her. Thank you for being so patient and kind. She needs that right now."

He acknowledged her with a short nod. "I just want to find this—" he bit back the swear word and amended the sentiment with difficulty "—predator. I'm starting to get a clearer picture of who this guy is."

"Really?" she asked, surprised. "How so?"

"It's the little things. The details. In both attacks he wore fancy shoes, which suggests he works a job that requires an education. He's not blue collar. That's something. The fact that he didn't think to change his shoes says he's either cocky or sloppy and I think it's cockiness. He doesn't think he's going to get caught, which tells me he's done this more than a few times. He knows what he's doing and he's gotten familiar with the routine. But with cockiness comes mistakes. His arrogance will trip him up."

Iris shivered. "That means he's not going to stop."

"Yeah," he admitted, catching the way her pupils

dilated with the fear she couldn't hide. He wanted to fold her in his arms but he didn't. He stayed rooted to the spot. "But I'm on to him this time. When he screws up...I'll be there to catch him."

Chapter 14

Iris stepped into Dr. Seryn's cozy studio, her nerves strung tight as razor wire. Several times during the drive she considered turning around but when she thought of Sierra it buoyed her courage.

Now she was here and there was no turning back.

Dr. Seryn smiled warmly as she ushered her into the studio. "I'm so happy you came." She gestured to a chair, not the chaise, and Iris felt immediate, if not an inordinate amount of, relief. She knew this was silly because she was going to end up there anyway once the session started. "I wasn't sure if you were ready from the last time we spoke."

"I wasn't," Iris confessed, rubbing her arms briskly as a chill dusted her body even though it was comfortably warm in the studio. "But a young girl was hurt, too, and I feel I can't in good conscience let fear of what's locked in my head stop me from doing everything I can to bring this monster to justice."

"You're very much a protector," Dr. Seryn murmured. "It's easy to see why Sundance thinks so highly of you."

Iris did a double take. She hadn't expected to talk of Sundance. "What do you mean? What has he said?"

Dr. Seryn smiled. "All good things."

"Could you be more specific?" Iris asked, feeling compelled to explain. "We haven't always been close. In fact, once he actually called me the bane of his existence so you can understand why I find it difficult to grasp his change of heart."

Dr. Seryn shrugged. "Well, all he's ever said about you is how good, strong and loyal you are. In my book, those are good things. Yes?"

Iris, remembering how kind he'd been as of late, smiled a bit shyly. "Yeah, those are good things."

"I agree. Let's focus on that for now. So, shall we get started?"

Jitters returning, Iris nonetheless nodded. "It's now or never. Do I have to lay on that chaise?"

"Not at all. If you're uncomfortable in the chaise you can stay where you are. The chair you're in has a mild recline so feel free to lean back to your preference."

"I guess we can't do this standing up?"

Dr. Seryn smiled indulgently. "Not the way I do it." Iris eased back in the chair with a sigh. Dr. Seryn waited until Iris was settled, then said, "I'm going to record our session so that you can take it with you and play it at home. Hypnosis works best with repetition in the meditative state. And often you're more comfortable in your home environment, making it easier to reach those theta brain waves."

Iris closed her eyes, determined to succeed at this for Sierra's sake, even if she was leery about the process and the science.

The melody and cadence of Dr. Seryn's voice soon lulled her into a relaxed state and Iris's muscles lost the tension she'd been carrying around for a month. It felt good to sink into the soft cushions and focus on something other than her trauma. Dr. Seryn led her down an imaginary staircase and into a beautiful place in her mind where it was safe and peaceful. Once there, Dr. Seryn asked her to go back to the night she went to The Dam Beaver for karaoke night.

"What are you wearing?" she asked.

Iris smiled. "My favorite going-out top. It's a tight pink V-neck. My hair is down and curled at the ends. The music is loud. The bar is hopping."

"Are there lots of people?"

"Yes. Karaoke is popular."

"Did you sing, too?"

"Yes."

"What did you sing?"

"'I Hate Myself for Loving You' by Joan Jett."

"Are you singing it to anyone in particular? Someone at the bar?"

"Not at the bar. Sundance hates karaoke."

"What else do you see?"

Iris floated over the scene in the bar that night, apart from the action, yet taking in everything. She saw Butch, the bartender/owner slinging drinks as fast as he could pour them. Karaoke night was a big moneymaker. People needed liquid courage to get onstage to embarrass themselves in front of an audience. A man to her left was leaning in, whispering in her ear. She was tipsy and enjoying the attention. Iris didn't know him but he was attractive and she liked that he kept buying her drinks.

"What do you see, Iris?"

"A man."

"What does the man look like? Do you know him?"

She shook her head. "I don't recognize him. He seems nice. Buys me drinks all night. I tell him I need to stop so I can drive later. He laughs and buys me another."

"Do you drink it?"

"Yes. I figure I can call Mya if I really shouldn't drive by the end of the night."

"Does he touch you at all?"

Iris's frown deepened and her heart rate kicked up a bit. "I…I don't know."

"That's okay. What does he look like? Can you describe him to me?"

"Tall, dark hair, looks my age. A little bit of scruff on his chin."

"Are you attracted to him? It's okay if you are."

"He's nice but he won't stop buying me drinks."

"Do you feel threatened?"

"No…maybe a little annoyed…"

"Can you remember his name?"

A voice in her ear floated from her memory as Iris said, "Brett. His name is Brett."

Sundance was finishing paperwork on a poaching case when Iris walked through his door. Her cheeks were dusted with pink and her brown eyes blazed with wild intense energy. For a moment he was so caught off guard by his body's reaction to seeing her that he almost missed what she was saying but finally the words "I might've come across something useful" sank in, and he had to give himself a mental shake to focus when he realized she was talking about the case.

"Yeah? Were you with Dr. Seryn today?"

"Yes," she answered, impatient to get to the point. "I remembered a name and a face."

That got his attention fast. He grabbed a pen and paper. "Go ahead."

"Tall, dark hair, about the same age as me, with some scruff on his chin, like a manicured goatee. And his name is Brett. Do you know of anyone that fits that description?"

Grant guy. "Yeah, I do. A guy by the name of Brett Duncan fits that description. He's the new grant man Chad brought in to find government grants for the relocation effort. I caught him chatting up Sierra the day before she was attacked. Thought it was inappropriate at the time but Chad assured me he was clean as a whistle. Not that I took his word for it. But, unfortunately, his wife gave him an alibi. According to her, he was sleeping soundly beside her, just as he'd claimed."

"Wives lie for their husbands," Iris said.

"And sometimes husbands lie to their wives. I think it's time to revisit Mr. Duncan and see what he remembers of the night when he was supposed to be sleeping beside his wife."

Iris smiled tremulously. "Do you think it could be him?"

He grabbed his keys. "I've never liked him. Something about the man seems wrong but I'll see what I can shake out of him." Sundance locked up and they walked to their vehicles. He was anxious to question Brett Duncan but he wasn't quite ready to jump in the Durango without talking to Iris about her session. "Did you recall anything else?" he asked carefully.

She shook her head. "It's still a blank spot but Dr. Seryn recorded our session on CD so I could do some work on my own. She said I might be able to break through after a few more sessions. But a name is a good start, right?"

"You bet it is. It's more than we had yesterday," he agreed solemnly, and she rewarded him with a shy smile. "You off for the day?"

Iris nodded. "I didn't know how this hypnosis stuff worked so I figured it was probably best to take the day off."

"You want to grab a bite to eat or something later?" he asked, not quite sure what he was doing. He had no business asking her out. She'd been through a traumatic experience. He tacked on "To talk about the case" before she had the chance to answer. The light in her eyes dimmed and he realized, somehow, he'd said the wrong thing. Her veiled disappointment poked at him but he wasn't sure how to fix it. "It was just a suggestion but you're probably tired. I'll let you know what I find out when I talk with Duncan."

"Sundance, wait," she called out as he climbed into his Durango. He paused, his stomach somewhere near his throat. She licked her lips, the full pout of her mouth drawing his attention before he could stop it. She ventured hesitantly, "You could stop by my place. I still have more casseroles than I could ever eat in my lifetime. I think Mya thought I was going to hibernate for the winter and she prepared appropriately. Either that or she's on a mission to make me fat so she can raid my closet with impunity," she added with a hint of her former dry humor.

It was on the tip of his tongue to decline—it'd been foolish to start down this path—but he liked the idea of spending more time with her, even if it was spent talking about the case. "A casserole sounds good. Mya is a good cook. Anything she makes tastes great."

"Yeah, unlike me who has a tendency to burn everything," she quipped.

He managed a grin. "See you tonight. Around sixish?"

Iris nodded and even returned a small smile. "Sixish. Come with your appetite."

"I will," he promised, though silently he wondered which appetite he truly wanted sated.

Sundance went straight to the Tribal Center. When Chad saw him coming, Sundance's expression no doubt dark and dangerous, he rushed from his office to delay him.

"Where's the fire?" he asked, concerned. "You've got murder in your eyes. Somehow I doubt that whatever you've got on your mind is good for your career. Let's chat in my office first."

"Where's Duncan?" he asked, ignoring Chad's offer, eager to put the grant guy under a hot bulb. "I have questions for him."

"He left early. Something about his wife, sick or something. What's wrong?"

"He failed to mention that he'd been with Iris the night she was attacked, tried to get her drunk. I want to know why he thought that wasn't important enough to mention."

Chad's expression faltered, as if caught between a rock and a hard place and he gestured for Sundance to follow him. Since Duncan was already gone, he blew out a breath in frustration and trailed Chad into his office. Chad leaned against his desk, setting his rump against the ledge, saying, "Here's the thing, Brett and his wife…I think they're having problems. Brett said he needed a drink and I didn't think he ought to be out by himself. I went with him to the bar that night but I never saw him with Iris."

Sundance narrowed his stare at Chad. "You never told me you were at the bar, too."

"You never asked. I didn't think it was relevant. I didn't end up staying. In spite of my good intentions, I must've eaten something bad because I left early with a sick gut."

"So you don't know what time Brett Duncan left the bar then?"

"Not exactly but I talked to Brett the next day and he said he didn't stay long."

Sundance's mouth firmed. Chad was trying to protect his employee but in Sundance's opinion, Brett Duncan was a prime suspect. And for that matter, Sundance realized with a sinking heart, so was Chad. "I still want to talk to him. I need his address."

Chad appeared resigned and supplied an address off the reservation. "For what it's worth…I don't think Brett is capable of what happened to Sierra or Iris. He's as soft as a marshmallow inside. He shuffles paper and stares at a computer all day."

Sundance allowed a short, tight smile. "Isn't that what you do?"

"Guilty," Chad admitted, then met Sundance's stare head-on, adding with self-assured conviction, "And I'm not into raping women, either. Just not my style, you know? Come on, Sundance. Guys like you and me… we don't have a problem getting a woman into our bed. It's just a fact." Sundance shifted, not sure how to feel about being lumped up in Chad's assessment but the sun was fading fast and he was supposed to be at Iris's house soon. Chad pushed off the desk. "I can tell you're hell-bent on questioning Brett so I'll just stay out of your way. I'm sure you can catch him at home tomorrow. In the meantime, it's quitting time for me. My dad is coming in tomorrow to tour the clinic and I get to play tour guide."

Sundance looked at him sharply, bothered by this bit of news. "I thought your dad put you in this position so he didn't have to travel to the reservations so much."

Chad shrugged. "I've long ago stopped trying to unravel why my father does anything. Maybe he's feeling nostalgic or maybe he wants to see what all the fuss is about. He's getting a lot of pressure high up about the flood situation. He wants to see how stretched thin the resources are here."

Sundance worried about Mya and Iris but he couldn't think of a good enough reason, that didn't sound suspect, to keep them away from Paul, until he said, "If he wants to see the true issues firsthand I'd be happy to take him to the flooded areas, show him where the houses used to stand. He might find that compelling enough evidence of a problem."

Chad waved away his offer. "Nah, he's hell-bent on seeing the clinic. I figure we'll spend a little time there and then I'll take him to lunch. The man loves food, women and drink—and not necessarily in that order. In the meantime—" Chad clapped Sundance on the shoulder good-naturedly "—good luck finding the bad guy. You're nothing if not tenacious. I'll give you that."

Sundance accepted the compliment, but his gut remained unsettled. He had questions circling in his brain but they'd have to wait until tomorrow.

He watched as Chad exchanged light banter with everyone on his way out. Sundance was bothered by the fact that Chad had also failed to mention he was at the bar that night with Iris. Having a drink wasn't a crime, but Sundance would've felt a whole lot more secure if Chad had been forthright from the beginning.

Sundance climbed into his truck, his thoughts grim.

Brett Duncan wasn't the only person Sundance needed to question further.

Chad Brown had just been added to the list.

The question that nagged at him...should he add Paul Brown to the list, too?

His shoulders tensed at the thought of going after a man high up in the food chain in the BIA, but he'd do it if he had to.

Whoever this person was...they messed with the wrong people.

Chapter 15

Iris smoothed the fancy tablecloth covering her not-so-fancy dining room table and wondered—again—what she was thinking inviting Sundance over as if they were at the very least friends and not two people caught up in a really messed-up situation.

There was no denying that if she hadn't been attacked, Sundance probably wouldn't have wasted much time looking in her direction unless it was to make some remark about her behavior and how ridiculous she was being at any given moment.

Of course, that being the case she most likely would've told him to go somewhere private and pull the stick out of his butt.

She smiled at that but her nerves were still a mess. She'd been out of her mind inviting him to dinner. A glance at the clock revealed little time to back out and cancel.

Rats.

And with impeccable timing, a knock sounded at the door, nearly causing her to jump out of her skin.

Saaski rose from his spot near the wood burning stove and followed her to the door, his coal-black eyes intent on who was behind it. She gave him a reassuring scratch behind the ears and, after checking to ensure it was indeed Sundance, she opened the door with a shaky smile.

"Hope you're hungry," she said, her nervousness showing. She dropped the grin and gestured toward the dining room table. "I popped a lasagna in the oven so I hope you like that sort of thing. I figured it was a fair guess that you would, seeing as Mya made it. Didn't she do all the cooking when you were kids?"

He shrugged out of his thick jacket and set it aside, his gaze oddly bright. "I like lasagna just fine. You know, you didn't have to do this—"

"I know that," she said too quickly, her heart rate tripling for a beat. Oh, for heaven's sake…was this a preview for the entire evening? Both of them dancing around the awkward silence and stilted conversation? She drew a deep breath and offered a determined smile as she took a seat, indicating he should do the same, which he did. Iris took the lead and dished herself a modest serving. Her appetite hadn't quite returned yet but she was doing her best to keep eating before she dropped another ten pounds and none of her clothes fit. She waited for him to dish up and take a bite. "It's good, right?"

"As ever. Mya's lasagna is my favorite."

I may have already known that, she thought with a flush. "I can't cook like this," she blurted out.

And by his expression, he already knew that. "Good

information to know if I ever have the notion of asking you to cook me something."

She stuffed a large bite in her mouth before she said something equally lame for the sake of filling the silence. She risked a look at him and her heart squeezed. Why did he have to be so handsome? *When* had he become so amazing? Of course, she would be doomed to fall head over heels for someone who saw her as nothing more than an obligation—

"I tried to talk with Brett Duncan today but he'd already left the office." Sundance broke into her thoughts, totally unaware of the inner dialogue turning her delicious meal into sawdust in her mouth. He frowned as if something were troubling him, then said, "Do you remember seeing Chad Brown, the new liaison at the Tribal Center at the bar that night? He said he was with Brett but he hadn't mentioned that he saw you."

She tried not to let her disappointment show that he only wanted to discuss the case. She swallowed her bite and searched her memory but came up empty. "I don't remember him, but then, I hadn't met him yet. He could've been there. The bar was wall-to-wall people and it was hard to pick out familiar faces much less those of strangers."

Sundance nodded. "I don't like that he didn't volunteer the information," he admitted.

"Yeah…but to be fair, why would he? I mean, do you always volunteer your whereabouts to people?"

"I'm not just some random person. He knows I'm investigating this case. He should've said something."

"Perhaps," she allowed, then added with a slight frown, "He doesn't seem the type to frequent The Dam Beaver. I don't know him very well but he seems…I don't know, like a guy with soft hands." She remembered

Chad from her brush with him at the hospital when he came to visit Sierra and recalled her initial wariness around him. It was on the tip of her tongue to share her first impression of Chad with Sundance, but given the fact that her reaction was likely the result of her trauma, she kept it to herself. It was bad enough Sundance saw her only as a victim, she needn't compound the situation by confirming that she was damaged. "I'm surprised you and him remained friends all this time. He doesn't seem the type you'd want to hang out with."

Sundance shrugged. "He made me laugh and we had some good times. After he left, we ended up like pen pals, I guess. I didn't actually physically see him again until after high school."

"Has he changed much from what you remember?"

Sundance gave it some thought before admitting, "I'm not sure. I mean, everyone changes to some degree. He still makes me laugh, if that counts for something."

She smiled, but uncertainty remained even if she'd made the decision to keep it to herself.

Sundance continued, ignorant of her personal quandary. "He's helping me out with the bigwigs in the Bureau of Indian Affairs department. I respect anyone who wants to fight on the side of the Native Americans for better treatment, services or whatever it happens to be. He seems to care more than most."

"And why is that?" she asked, unable to help herself. "He isn't Hoh, right? Why does he care so much?"

"I don't know. I think he feels an affinity for the land here. He's not Hoh but he's Native American of some sort, I think. Never thought to ask. But he seems to care. And he's doing a lot of work behind the scenes to help address some of the issues that have been pushed aside on the federal level. He's a man who gets things done and I like that."

She digested the information and finally agreed silently that her initial impression of the man had to have been colored by her experience, which made her feel alternately depressed and guilty. She supposed she ought to apologize to Chad at some point for her rudeness the last time they spoke. Iris toyed with her fork, idly wondering if she'd ever be normal again. She caught Sundance's steady gaze and when she saw something other than professional courtesy, her breath hitched in her chest. She managed to swallow but felt terribly exposed by that gaze. His almond-shaped, deep-set eyes were never something she'd imagined would set her heart to fluttering, but when he was looking at her like he was, she found it hard to breathe.

"I wish you'd never been at that bar," he said, shocking her with his quiet admission.

How many times had she thought the very same thing? Wishing she'd opted to stay home that night, quietly munching on frozen pizza and washing it down with a beer or two? Enough times to realize that her wishing was a depressing waste of time.

She flashed a short smile before pushing away her plate, unable to force another bit. "Me, too. But if it hadn't been me, it would've been someone else and it eats me up inside that Sierra is going through what I am. It's hard. Every day is a struggle to find myself," Iris said, not surprised when her nose tingled, signaling tears weren't far behind. "But I'm not giving up. I have to believe that it gets better…somehow."

"I have to believe that, too."

A watery smile followed as she said, "Yeah?"

"Yeah. It eats at me, my failure."

"You haven't failed at anything, Sonny," she said, overwhelmed by the desire to touch him, even if only to grasp his hand and squeeze it for the pain she glimpsed in his stare. This was a side of Sundance she'd never seen and it humbled her beyond anything she could have imagined. "This wasn't your fault. You can't be everywhere at once. Everyone knows you'd do anything to protect your people." She held his stare, adding softly, "I don't blame you for this…I never would."

Sundance felt as if his chest was being squeezed by an invisible hand, as if something large had reached inside his rib cage and twisted his heart until it stuttered to a stop. He wanted to tell her that he'd known she was going to the bar that night, that Mya had told him, had actually suggested that he stop by and say hello. He'd turned Mya down, stating stiffly that he had to work and it wouldn't be appropriate. But in truth, he had been unable to stop himself. On the pretense of going to a call nearby, he actually had peeked into the bar, his gaze going straight and steady to Iris. He could hear her laughter as she danced, enjoying herself with the kind of abandon he'd come to expect from her. Men were never far from her side, each more eager than the last to gain her attention but, though she accepted their drinks and flattery, she gave them nothing in return. It used to make him roll his eyes, but lately it had made him burn with something he didn't recognize to know all those men wanted a piece of the hot-blooded woman. Including himself.

And when he'd realized he couldn't pretend not to care this time, he'd walked right back out.

He should've stayed. By leaving he'd left her with a predator.

Sundance pulled away but his sense of bone-deep guilt remained. "I'll find who did this," he vowed, needing to say something, anything to ease the ache in his heart. "I don't care how long it takes. I'll find who did this to you and Sierra."

"I know you will," Iris said without a hint of reservation. Her faith in him kept him from drowning and renewed his determination to succeed. She broke out into a smile and gathered their plates. He rose to help. Without asking, she sectioned out some of the leftovers for him to take home. Her consideration loosened the tension knotting his body. Saaski trotted over and she gave him a treat. Sundance watched, pleased to see how well both the dog and Iris took to one another. He'd done one thing right, at the very least. They worked beside one another, making small talk as they made short work of cleaning up after their meal and Sundance found deep satisfaction in the simple, domestic task. Most men were stunned by Iris's beauty when she had her "face" on as she called it. But Sundance had never much cared for all that goop mucking up what was already perfect. And now, with her clean skin, hair down and loose, even wearing soft, worn leggings and an oversize sweater, she was more beautiful than ever. He imagined touching her smooth skin, tasting her supple lips and allowing her hair to slide through this fingertips. Realizing he'd momentarily checked out, lost in thoughts best left alone, he found Iris watching him with uncertainty.

"Is something wrong?" she asked.

He ought to lie. But he couldn't. Iris deserved honesty even if he didn't know how to form the words without bungling his intention. He'd never been good at the touchy-feely stuff. Mya was the sensitive one in the family. He'd always been counted upon for the muscle and the cool head; that didn't help him much at the moment. He forced a grin. "It's nothing, just a million thoughts buzzing through my head," he said, annoyed at himself for being such a coward. He didn't know how to act around Iris when he wasn't fulfilling a preordained role. Historically, they'd disliked each other immensely. In the past, they'd spar verbally and then go their separate ways, grumbling about the other to whoever would listen—most often Mya.

"I can't imagine the burden you bear for the tribe," Iris said, misinterpreting his statement. "Are you having any luck getting funds for another officer?"

"Ah, maybe. It's too early to tell but that's one of the things Chad's been helping with." His thoughts tripped to Paul Brown and his visit to the clinic tomorrow and he knew he couldn't remain quiet. "Listen, Chad is going to stop by the clinic tomorrow to give his father, Paul, a tour. I'll be honest, I don't like the guy. On the surface he and Chad share that same 'I'm a likable guy' quality but it seems like an act with Paul."

"Well, he's a federal guy. What can you expect?" Iris quipped, not particularly concerned.

"He wasn't always a fed guy," he shared, earning a frown from Iris. "Apparently, he used to be a vet, of all things."

"That's an odd leap in career choices."

"Yeah…"

"So why don't you like him?"

He shrugged. "Just a gut thing." Iris seemed to understand but didn't share her own thoughts. He took that to mean she believed he was overreacting a bit, and maybe he was. This case had him jumping at shadows, suspecting the worst of everyone. Even so, he'd feel a lot more secure knowing Iris and his sister would be on their guard around the man. "Would you mind telling Mya to keep her distance? At least for now until I can get a better handle on things."

"Sure," she said, but her gaze remained troubled. Her mouth pinched, almost involuntarily but she covered quickly as if determined to change her mind about something. "We haven't talked much about the case," she noted, a faint worry line appearing in her forehead. "I know you wanted to hear about my session with Dr. Seryn."

"Do you feel okay about her now?" he asked.

She smiled. "Yeah. It's not what I thought it was going to be like. A lot less intimidating now that I know what I'm going to be doing."

"How are you coping with the stuff that's coming back to you?"

She stilled and the easy smile faded. "I haven't really had any major flashbacks aside from the memory of that guy Brett. Dr. Seryn said that I might have them after repeated sessions."

"If you need anything…"

"Thanks."

More silence followed and he realized he should go before he said or did something he shouldn't. "Dinner hit the spot. Most times I eat a sandwich or a bowl of cereal."

"I can't imagine Mya doesn't keep you stocked with casseroles, too," Iris teased lightly. "The woman loves to mother."

He smiled. "She's a good woman. Someday she'll make someone a good wife."

Iris made a face. "And there you go, sounding like the Sundance I know and remember," she said, though there was a hint of laughter in her voice.

"What did I say?"

"It's that old-fashioned attitude that women's values are equal to their domestic skills. Your sister is a talented doctor who keeps this reservation going strong with much personal sacrifice yet you can only find praise in the way she can run a household. Sonny…shame on you," she chided. "Not all women were cut out for the kitchen, you know."

"I know that," he retorted, enjoying the spark kindling to life in her eyes. It was a light he hadn't seen since the attack. "And thank Great Spirit for that. Otherwise, who would do the laundry?"

She gasped and tossed an oven mitt his way. He ducked in time but not before the second volley of a damp dish towel landed in his face. He pulled it away and lobbed it back at her. She laughed and caught it, her reflexes quick as a cat. Her eyes sparkled with amusement and he drank in the sight like a man dying of thirst. He hadn't realized how much he'd come to enjoy their little "battles." Only now, he wished he had the right to pull her into his arms and wage a different kind of confrontation, one that ended with someone on top. His groin warmed as the thought manifested into imagery in his head. He shook it off with effort and reached for the packaged leftovers. The best thing, the smart thing, was to end on a high note. She'd been through a lot; she certainly didn't need him pawing at her.

When she realized he was ready to leave, her bottom lip caught under her front teeth and he could've sworn he read disappointment but it was gone in a minute. "Thank you for your company tonight. It was nice."

"Yeah, it was," he agreed. "Maybe we can do it again," he suggested, testing the waters. When she didn't quip something offhandedly negative at the idea, he felt a jump of excitement that he was selfish enough to savor. He hefted the warm container of leftovers in his hand. It was time for him to walk away, yet he continued to search for a reason to stay. She was close enough he could reach out and circle her waist to pull her to him. He could almost feel the heat of her body against his. He swallowed with difficulty, an appetite for something aside from sustenance fueling his thoughts. She seemed to note the difference in his body language. Her pupils, dilating as her breath hitched, made her eyes black as night.

"Sundance?" she asked, a wealth of uncertainty in her soft voice.

"I—" What could he say? *I haven't always treated you right but I think I may have fallen in love with you a while back and now I don't know how to tell you?* Yeah, that would go over well. Get it together! Forcing a grin, he said, "I really appreciate the food. Mya's always after me to eat better. Now I can say I have."

She returned the smile but clearly she'd expected something else. "It's the least I can do," she murmured, seeing him to the door, adding once he'd cleared the threshold, "Drive safe."

He stalked to his Durango, his thoughts in a mess as frustration ate at him. If he'd had the balls to tell her how he'd felt before she was attacked, none of this would have happened to her because she wouldn't have been at that bar alone.

His only hope for redemption was to find that son of a bitch and put him away.

Or put him in the ground.

And then? He'd figure that out later.

Chapter 16

A familiar well of disappointment and sadness bubbled to the surface as she watched Sundance pull away. For a breathless moment, she'd been sure Sundance was going to kiss her. Of course, that was ludicrous. Mya's conversation came back to her about Sundance caring for her as more than just a tribal member, but she couldn't fathom the possibility. He'd never looked twice in her direction before the attack. If anything he'd been more distant than ever. Nothing she'd tried from her female arsenal had worked. He'd been immune to flirting, teasing, blatant suggestion—everything had been met with cool disinterest.

She let herself sink into the sofa, her head falling against the plush cushion with a heavy sigh. Saaski pushed his way between her legs to rest his big head on her thigh. She smiled with true adoration and pride. This dog was the best gift anyone had ever given her.

She gave him a good scratch along his rib cage. "Tell me what I should do, you big, scary, beautiful canine," she murmured. But Saaski merely whined and licked his chops and she chuckled. "All right, I'll get you a treat but then it's straight to bed for you and me."

She rose and grabbed Saaski a jerky treat. As she passed the counter she saw the hypnosis CD Dr. Seryn had made for her at their last session and stopped. The night sounds penetrated the small house and she realized if she ever wanted to be free from this hell, she had to take steps.

She eyed the CD. The possibility that the identity of her attacker was locked in her head was a scary thing. But Iris refused to live in fear for her entire life. She scooped up the CD and walked resolutely to her bedroom, Saaski on her heels. She changed into her night clothes and, after rooting around to find her CD player, she settled into her bed with her headphones on.

She allowed her eyes to close, the intimate sound of Dr. Seryn's smooth, soft voice in her ear, soothing her fears and renewing her determination to succeed.

Soon, from the safety of her mind, she returned to the bar in her memory.

The music, the people, the smells, even the taste of the beer on her tongue—all of it came back to her. She heard her own flirty laughter, watched as she danced and sang, remembered that she'd been wishing Sundance were there to see her.

Midnight was approaching. She'd made the decision to call it a night. Someone was urging her to have another drink. She declined but laughed as she said it, definitely sounding as if she could easily be persuaded to change her mind. Her bladder was full to the point of pain. She needed to pee. She disappeared to the ladies' restroom, intent on leaving after she relieved herself. She returned to take a small sip of her tonic spritzer and noticed it had tasted bitter. The guy who'd been buying her drinks all night was gone, had moved on. She could see him zeroing in on someone else, someone more likely to put out.

Dizziness started to cloud her vision. She gripped the bar to steady herself. Someone asked if she was all right. She waved away their concern; she was fine. Just a little woozy. Probably should call Mya to come get her. Her stomach felt queasy, unsettled.

A hand on her arm held her upright as her knees started to weaken. A part of her couldn't believe this was happening. She hadn't drank enough to be so incapable of standing. Her clinical training kicked in and a chill followed the realization that she'd been drugged. She had to find help. Her vision had begun to smear. She turned to find Butch but he was at the far end of the bar. There were faces she didn't know blurring into the fuzzy landscape.

Suddenly the gentle but firm pressure of a hand steadying her had her offering a slurred thank you as she was propelled from the crowded bar to the cold shock of outside.

"Drugged," she managed to say, needing this person to take her to the urgent care center.

A low rumble of soft laughter followed. She frowned, there was nothing funny about this. But the touch on her arm became painful and she stumbled in her attempt to free herself.

"So feisty," the voice murmured, easily deflecting her clumsy attempt to strike out at whoever was doing this to her. She was put into a car and strapped in. She pawed at the door handle, not quite able to manage enough strength to grip the cold plastic. Delighted laughter followed and she fought the urge to vomit. A hand on her hair, playing with the long strands, made her want to scream. "Oh, the things I'm going to do to you…"

And then there was nothing.

Sundance pulled up to the modest home outside of Forks and after a short, assessing look around, he knocked on the door. A petite blonde with chin-length hair answered with a smile. "Can I help you?"

Sundance flashed his credentials. "I'm Sundance Jonson, tribal police officer on the neighboring reservation where your husband works. We spoke on the phone," he reminded her.

Her expression cooled. "Yes. I already told you my husband was home that night."

He ignored her declaration and looked past her. "Is your husband home? He wasn't at the Tribal Center today and he left early yesterday."

"He's sick," she answered stiffly, preparing to close the door, but Sundance stopped her with the flat of his hand and a warning look.

"I need to speak with him. Now."

She swallowed, looking as if she wanted to slam the door in his face but resisted because she didn't want to go to jail for assault. But she knew something was up because she kept sending furtive glances behind her. Sundance gave the door a hard push, that knocked her out of the way and revealed Brett hiding in the foyer behind a large potted plant.

"You don't have the right to—"

He cut off the wife's tirade by zeroing in on Brett. "Is

there a reason you lied to me about your whereabouts the night Iris Beaudoin was attacked?"

"I didn't lie." He shared a look with his wife. "I was home sleeping."

"Yeah, that's what you said but I know that's a lie. And you and your wife both know that's a lie. What I figure is that you told her you were somewhere other than where you really were, that is why she's willing to fudge your whereabouts. But does she know that you were actually at the bar and trying to pick up the victim?"

"You were at the bar?" Brett's wife's voice rippled with hurt indignation. Sundance wondered what tale he'd spun to get her to lie for him. She'd clearly known her husband hadn't been in bed beside her that night. "You told me you were at a meeting! You told me to lie because you didn't want your boss to know you were moonlighting for extra cash! You liar!"

Brett blanched, his skin turning a sickly shade as he was clearly caught. His wife looked ready to cry. "Jana—"

"I knew you were lying," she stated, her eyes filling with tears. She turned to Sundance, saying with enough bitterness to reveal all wasn't right in the Duncan marriage, "I take back what I said. He wasn't with me. He didn't come home until 2:00 a.m." She turned to her husband and spat. "I didn't uproot my life so we could have a fresh start just so you could go back to your whoring ways. I want you out."

Brett wanted to go after her but with Sundance standing there, a silent witness to their little drama, he was stuck. He shot Sundance a nasty look but stayed put. "Are you happy? You just ruined my marriage."

Sundance's gaze narrowed as he gave the man a cold

smile. "We both know you weren't at a business meeting, unless you regularly hold meetings at The Dam Beaver. Let's try for the truth this time. Where were you between the hours of 10:00 p.m. and 1:00 a.m.?"

"Are you charging me with something?" Brett asked.

"Just answer the question."

"I'm not answering anything until I talk with my lawyer. If you're charging me with something, get on with it. If not, get out of my house. I have to talk with my wife."

Brett turned to follow in the direction of his wife but Sundance wasn't finished yet. He grabbed the man and spun him around, pinning him to the wall with his forearm against Brett's windpipe. "I don't think you heard me correctly," he said silkily, as the man struggled to breathe. "I want to know where the hell you were between the hours of 10:00 p.m. and 1:00 a.m. It's very simple. I don't care if you were banging some willing broad behind your wife's back. I just want to know if you were assaulting a woman who'd been drugged earlier at the bar. An eyewitness puts you at the scene with the victim. Now, I can drag your sorry, cheating ass down to the station but you should know by now that I work for a sovereign nation and our rules aren't the same as yours. So call your lawyer, but I can guarantee that if you're guilty, no lawyer is going to save you from the tribal justice that's going to rain down on your head. Are we clear?" Sundance let up on the man's throat and Brett drew in deep, wheezing breaths, fear registering in his eyes. Stepping away, Sundance gave the man a second to compose himself but he wasn't going anywhere until he got some answers. His adrenaline was kicking in his veins and it took every ounce of self-control he had not to pummel the answers out of the man.

Brett massaged his throat, his fear finally loosening his lips, and he lost the earlier bravado. "Yeah, I saw her. She was the hottest chick in the bar. Kinda hard to miss. I bought her a few drinks but when I realized I wasn't going to get anything for my trouble, I moved on around midnight or so." He did a quick check to make sure his wife's door was still closed tight and said in a lowered voice, "Listen, I went home with an older chick named Bonnie Sweet. She'll verify that I was with her until two. Then I came home."

Nice. Coming home to the wife after shagging some other woman. "So when did Chad Brown leave the bar?" he asked, not even trying to disguise his disgust for the man.

"He left earlier, I think. I don't know. I was pre-occupied and since we brought separate cars I wasn't worried about a ride."

"You two go out often?" Sundance inquired.

"Not really. This was our first time to the bar. I mean, he's my boss."

Until he questioned Bonnie Sweet to verify Brett's story, he'd have to let up. "If I find out you're lying to me again…I'll do more than leave a few bruises," he warned. By the way Brett's Adam's apple bobbed, the man believed him. He had one more question. "Where were you the night Sierra was attacked?"

"Home. With my wife."

"I've heard that before."

"This time I'm not lying." Brett swallowed, then added with earnest, "I know I shouldn't have lied the first time, but put yourself in my shoes…"

"I'm not a lying sack of crap who cheats on his wife,"

Sundance said. "So I can't imagine myself in your shoes. I don't care about your life or how you live it. I'm trying to solve a case. That's it. Don't lie to me and we'll get along just fine. But you've already tipped the scale against you so don't expect any favors." Brett wisely remained silent as Sundance saw himself to the door. He said, "I'll be in touch," and returned to his Durango. He could only imagine what was going to happen between those two after he left. Sundance hoped Brett's wife had the wherewithal to leave the sorry excuse for a husband but he didn't waste much more thought on the Duncans.

He had a feeling Brett's story would check out. Bonnie Sweet was a bit of a loose skirt on the reservation. Chances are she banged him just like he said, which would give Brett a solid—if not sleazy—alibi.

That left Chad.

Chad swore he'd left earlier that night.

But Sundance couldn't just take his word for it.

Hopefully, he had a solid alibi.

Because right about now, he was looking more and more like a suspect instead of an old friend.

Chapter 17

Sundance was preparing to confront Chad when the man walked through his front door at the station.

"We need to talk," Chad stated, his mouth grim. "I heard you went to Brett's house and roughed him up pretty good." When Sundance offered little reaction, Chad swore under his breath. "What are you doing, man? You can't go kicking people around like you're Sitting Bull or something. There's rules and laws for a reason and if you hope to keep your funding, you won't break or bend them for your own purposes."

"I'm running an investigation. He was a person of interest and he refused to answer my questions until I persuaded him to change his attitude. After that, he was cooperative."

Chad's mouth tightened and Sundance appreciated his position but the investigation was more important than political posturing in his world, so Chad would just have to deal with it.

"I'm glad you came by. I need to ask you some questions," Sundance said.

"Are you going to kick me around, too, to get what you need?" Chad asked, half joking.

"Depends on your answers," he retorted, not laughing.

"This sounds serious," Chad said, sighing as he grabbed a chair and made himself comfortable. "What can I do for you?"

"I need to know where you were between the hours of 10:00 p.m. and 1:00 a.m. the night Iris was attacked. And try to be specific."

Chad frowned. "Back to this? I told you where I was. Home, alone, barfing my guts out. It must've been something I ate. I felt better the next morning."

He wanted to take him at his word but if he were anyone else, he wouldn't. "Would you mind if I took a DNA sample to rule you out?"

"I didn't know DNA had been collected from the victims," Chad said with mild interest. Sundance refrained from elaborating, just waited for Chad's consent, that he didn't get. Chad exhaled and shook his head. "I want to help you out, I mean, I want whoever did this caught as much as you do but I gotta tell you, I'm starting to get a real 'you're a suspect' vibe from you. Is there something I ought to know? I'm just a paper pusher, like you said. Do I really look like the kind of man who preys on women?"

"It's not personal," Sundance said. "You don't have an alibi for that night. You and Brett both failed to disclose that you were at the bar with the victim. You're both off-rez and I can't ignore the fact that you're both new to the area."

"Come on, Sundance…there had to have been plenty of off-rez people in that bar that night. Are you going to run down every single person and ask them to spit on a stick so you can run their DNA? I'm pretty sure that's an invasion of privacy, even in these liberal times. And I'm not entirely off-rez having lived here for seven years in the past. Doesn't that count for something?"

"Are you saying no?" Sundance asked, hating that Chad was being resistant.

"I am—for now—but I hate to think that you might believe me capable of rape so I'm going to level with you," Chad said, looking uncomfortable. "Here's the honest to God's truth and it isn't something I'm proud of…" He drew a deep breath, shaking his head as if unable to believe he was about to share. "I have proof I was home at the hours in question."

"How so? I thought you said you were alone."

"Well, I said there was no one at the house with me."

"Sounds like alone in my book."

"It is if you're not online with someone."

Sundance stared. "Come again?" he asked.

"Okay, it's true I went home sick after the bar but after I threw up I felt better…and a little lonely, if you catch my drift. I hadn't expected to go home so early and…well, there's this website I frequent when the action's been a little on the slow side."

"Are you talking about porn?" Sundance asked, trying not to let his surprise show.

Chad colored. "Yeah." An awkward pause followed, and then he said, "Anyway, it's a pay and play kind of thing and I can bring you a copy of my credit card statement that shows when and how long I was on the site."

Sundance smiled, a flood of relief lightening his voice as he said, "If you can get me that copy, I think I can do without your DNA. Sorry, but I had to ask."

"You're just doing your job. I appreciate that. Hell, I know if I'm ever the victim of a crime, I want you on the case. You don't give up."

"No, I don't," Sundance said. "I can't. These are my people and I will catch whoever did this."

"So how'd you come up with new details? I thought the victims couldn't remember anything. Something about the drug caused some sort of amnesia."

"True but one of them is using hypnosis and new details are coming out. Sooner or later, a detail will emerge that will crack this case wide-open. I have a feeling."

Chad smiled. "Great. Tell her to stick with it. I hope it works out."

"Me, too."

Chad unfolded himself from the chair. "Well, if you're finished grilling me, I need to head back to the office."

He walked Chad to the door. "I'm sorry for the questions."

Chad grinned. "Never feel the need to apologize for doing your job. The world needs more people like you. You'd be surprised how many would've just ignored their instincts for the sake of preserving a relationship. You do good work."

"How'd the tour of the clinic go with your father?" he asked.

Chad sighed and shrugged. "Fine. I was a bit disappointed, I didn't get to introduce him to Mya or Iris.

He would've benefited from hearing straight from them how it is at the clinic. But, apparently, we'd just missed them. Iris and Mya had gone to lunch together."

"Yeah, they're real close," Sundance said, secretly relieved.

"Yeah, I got that impression. All right, I'll let you get back to work. And I'll let you know what I hear from my father about the funding requests."

As relieved as Sundance was to scratch Chad from the suspect list, coupled with the fact that he grudgingly had to eliminate Brett as well, that left him with a big, fat zero, and Sundance hated knowing that he was back to square one in his investigation. He scrubbed his hands over his face, feeling every year of his life weighing down on him, pressing the air from his chest. He steepled his fingers before him, wondering where to go next.

Iris rounded a corner, her stomach growling a reminder that she'd passed the lunch hour at least a handful of hours ago, and nearly ran into Mya who was chatting with Chad Brown and another man she didn't recognize. Immediately her stomach muscles tensed and she was overwhelmed with the need to run but her reaction only served to piss her off and she forced a smile as she walked toward them.

"What's going on here?" she asked, looking to Mya who'd been giving Chad an almost flirty smile before she'd realized anyone was watching.

The older man stepped forward and grasped her hand in welcome. She forced a smile and resisted the urge to jerk her hand away. "We missed each other the other day and I felt a visit wouldn't be complete if I didn't meet the two women everyone says keep this place running like a well-oiled machine. My name's Paul Brown, director of Indian affairs, at your service."

She risked a short look at Mya, communicating that this was the man Sundance had warned them about but Mya didn't seem to catch the hint. She was too focused on the fact that this man—a man of power—had taken a real interest in her clinic. And since the clinic could use someone in high places in its corner, she was more than willing to play nice. "Pleased to meet you," she murmured, pulling her hand free as soon as it was polite.

"Are all the nurses and doctors as pretty as you two?" he asked with a wink that shot way past the mark of inappropriate, but Mya seemed willing to overlook it for the moment.

"Dad, you're embarrassing yourself," Chad said, earning a small point in his favor from Iris. "These ladies are more than pretty faces, they're the backbone of this operation. Let's be respectful."

Mya smiled. "I'd be happy to show you around. I'm sorry we missed you yesterday," she said, shooting Iris a look that said, "don't be such a worrywart," and moved away, encouraging Paul to follow, which he was only too happy to. "We are in sore need of updated equipment in our OB department and our X-ray machine is straight out of the dark ages of medicine."

Iris opened her mouth to protest but Chad swooped in quickly. "She smells federal dollars. We've lost her," he joked but Iris couldn't dispel the tightness in her chest. Sundance didn't like the guy, he surely wouldn't want his sister traipsing off with him but what could she do? She returned to Chad, unable to hide the distress she felt. It was then she noticed the big bouquet of flowers behind his back. He noted her confusion and explained with a shrug. "Dad wanted to make a grand gesture. I told him I already brought Sierra flowers but he thought it might look good to bring another bunch from the BIA. You know, the personal touch."

"Sierra's not here," she said, trying not to let her personal feelings seep out too much.

"Yeah, we figured that out. A shame. These ones are much prettier than the ones I got her." He leaned forward to whisper conspiratorially, "He's got a bigger expense account." He produced the bouquet and thrust them at her, causing her to blink in surprise. "No sense in letting them go to waste. My dad was right about one thing, you are a beautiful woman. And beautiful women deserve flowers."

Iris accepted the flowers, unsure of how to feel about the unexpected gesture. Surely she was overreacting. What would the old Iris do in this situation? She'd gleefully accept the flowers with a cheeky grin and flirt shamelessly. She felt miles away from that woman. She stifled a frustrated groan at the niggling little voice that never seemed to shut up these days, particularly when the opposite sex was involved. At this rate, she'd be a card-carrying lesbian by the end of the month. Sundance was right, this case was turning everyone upside down. "They're lovely, thank you." She bit her bottom lip, her stomach choosing that moment to be particularly loud. She barked an embarrassed laugh, rubbing her belly. "Guess it's time to feed the beast after I put these in some water. Thanks again…"

She turned to leave but suddenly Chad seemed to have a grand idea, saying, "Hey, let's go together. Like you, I haven't eaten yet and seeing as my father has been kidnapped by Mya, that leaves you and me without someone to share lunch. I'm game if you are."

"I—" It was on the tip of her tongue to decline but she wasn't sure if she was saying no because she really didn't want to go or because she was afraid to be alone with a stranger. He was harmless, she told herself. Stop being ruled by fear, she chastised herself. Just say yes! "O-okay," she stammered, her cheeks flushing. Lifting her chin, she said in a stronger voice, "I'll go get my coat. We can walk to the deli cart."

"Ohhh, a deli cart. Sounds delicious," Chad said, teasing.

She knew for a fact no matter how sternly she might tell herself to get it together, there was no way she could climb into a car with a stranger so dining at the deli cart was all she could offer Chad Brown. She smiled angelically. "Take it or leave it. Today's special is chili in a bread bowl. My favorite."

"Well, lead on, Miss Iris. I'm your willing lunch companion, no matter what's on the menu."

Iris actually laughed and it felt good, almost as if she were catching a glimpse of her former self. Maybe she wouldn't become a lesbian after all. She paused to put the flowers in water and took a quick look at herself in the mirror as she shrugged on her coat. She looked the same, the bruises were long gone, and if she wanted to start feeling normal again, she'd have to start acting normal.

And she supposed that meant accepting lunch invitations from people outside of her inner circle. She resolutely pushed away the persistant feeling warning her of potential danger and pasted a smile on her face.

She would not be ruled by fear! It was just a chili bowl for goodness sakes.

Sundance caught Mya as she was cruising past the nurses' station, a patient history folder in hand. He called out to her and she smiled, gesturing for him to follow her into the staff lounge.

"What can I do for you, my brother?" she asked, closing the folder to give him her full attention. "You just missed Iris, she went to lunch with your friend Chad. Oh, and I had a lovely conversation with Paul Brown. I don't know why you wanted us to steer clear. He seems very nice, even if he's a little loose with what's considered politically correct." Startled by that, Sundance took a second to recover but Mya didn't seem to notice as she continued, "I like him. He's very charming. It seems the apple doesn't fall far from the tree with those Browns. I think Chad would be good for Iris."

"What?" he asked, annoyed at the idea and still uncomfortable with the fact that Paul Brown had made yet another unscheduled trip to the reservation. Seemed he'd taken quite a shine to the people and the place, which he found odd. If he'd liked it so much in the first place, why'd he leave? Added to that, he hated the fact that Iris was out with Chad. "She doesn't need to start dating anyone just yet. She needs to focus on healing and recovering."

Mya frowned. "And how do you think that's going to happen if she doesn't take baby steps toward being around the opposite sex? She's not made of china, Sonny. She can handle it. She's strong and determined to recover."

"And Chad is going to help her do that?"

"What's this? I thought Chad was your friend?"

Things change. But he couldn't rightly explain his feelings without bringing up the unsettling questions he was harboring so he changed the subject instead. "So where's Paul now?"

"I told him I had to finish rounds and passed him

off to the physician's assistant to show him the X-ray machine we're forced to work with. And back to the subject of Iris," she said, stubbornly refusing to let it go. "So what's the problem if Iris wants to get to know him better, maybe even go out with him? It's not as if the reservation is booming with eligible men. And it's not like you've declared your interest."

He scowled, absolutely hating the idea of Chad dating Iris but to admit that… It would reveal a lot more than he was willing to share at the moment. "I just think she needs to go slowly," he said.

Mya's expression warmed with love. "Oh, my sweet brother, always the protector. She's fine. Now, what did you need? Not that I don't love your visits, somehow I know this visit isn't social."

"I came to talk to Iris," he admitted, adding stiffly, "About the case."

Mya made a face, then sighed heavily. "Do you have a new lead?"

"No, the exact opposite. I'm back to ground zero. I need to speak with Iris and see if she's remembered anything new."

"I'm sure she would've told you if she had."

"Yeah," he acknowledged, hating the fact that he'd been more interested in seeing her than questioning her. "I wondered if she'd managed to try any of the self-hypnosis yet."

"I know a lot of my colleagues think it's a bunch of mumbo-jumbo but I don't know, I'm open to anything that might help," Mya said. "Just don't tell anyone I said that. My colleagues would tease me to death." Her smile faded as she added with a concerned frown, "Sonny, even though I'm not closed minded about hypnosis, I'm not sure it's a good idea to hang all your hopes on a pseudoscience. There's a good chance Iris simply won't remember, even with Emily's help, because of the drug she was given."

"I know but it's all I've got right now. Every other lead has dried up," he said, hating how desperate that admission made him feel. "So...where'd Iris and Chad go for lunch?"

Mya smiled, seeing right through him. He wasn't surprised, just annoyed at himself for trying. "They went to the deli cart. I'm sure you could catch them if you walk quickly."

He wanted to. His feet were already itching to move in that direction but he made himself shake his head. "No, that's okay. I can catch her later."

Mya gave a minute shake of her head and waved him off. "You're impossible," she declared, but softened her words with a warm smile. "Make sure you eat something, too. You're getting thin."

She left and he looked down to touch his stomach. That sounded like a good reason to eat a casserole with Iris. They could talk about the case then.

Satisfied with his plan, he almost had himself convinced that he didn't care that Iris was enjoying lunch with someone else.

Specifically, Chad Brown.

Chapter 18

Iris tried to remember to smile and act unaffected by the fact that inside she was shrinking.

"Are you cold?" Chad asked, mistaking her shiver for one caused by the chill in the air. He made a motion to shrug off his jacket but she waved away his concern.

"I'm fine," she assured him, forcing another smile that she hoped appeared bright and confident instead of nervous and agitated, which was how she felt. "So, Sundance tells me you're working on finding funding so that we can relocate some of the tribe members who are in the flood plain?"

"Guilty. I'm close, I think. But right now I'm really focusing on finding funding for more tribal officers. Poor Sundance is being run ragged."

Iris snuck a glance at Chad as she chewed her mouthful of chili. She wanted to loosen up but her chest felt tight and miserable and it was difficult to pretend otherwise.

"I'm bugging you, aren't I?" he asked, surprising her.

"No," she disagreed vehemently. "It's not you…I'm just preoccupied. My mind is elsewhere today." Make that every day. Don't take it personal, dude. "I'm sorry I'm not very good company."

He assessed her openly, which made her straighten and meet his stare head-on, though it took a fair amount of mental muscle not to cringe. "You've changed."

"Excuse me?" she said, going very still. "How do you know? To my knowledge we've only just met a few days ago."

He grinned, throwing her off. "I confess, I haven't known you long but I've seen you out and about. You're hard to miss."

She blushed, unsure how to accept the compliment. Before her attack, she would've grinned, preening from his admiration, but now? Panic was her go-to feeling and she hated it. "That's sweet of you. Where had you seen me? At the clinic?"

"No. I saw you at the bar. Unfortunately, it was the night of the attack."

Iris swallowed, her breath coming in short, shallow gasps. He started toward her and she took a quick step away. His immediate chagrin made her realize she was overreacting again. She shook her head, tears filling her eyes, as she tried to explain. "I have changed. I'm trying to find my way back but sometimes I can't help myself and the panic takes over. It's not personal," she said, wiping at her eyes. "It's something I'm trying to overcome but it's harder than I imagined it would be."

"I'm so sorry," he said. "I should've been more sensitive. I was a clod."

"No…it's not you, it's me." She smiled through her tears, even laughing at herself. "I used to be fearless. Mya used to call me reckless, even. Now I'm practically afraid of my shadow."

"I can only imagine what you're going through," he murmured. "I heard that you don't remember the actual attack. Perhaps that's a blessing…"

She hesitated, not quite comfortable discussing the case with a virtual stranger but she supposed she'd have to get used to people bringing it up at some point. She choked down the lump in her throat with difficulty, saying, "I used to think it was but I think the clue to finding who did this to me is locked in my head. I'm trying to unlock the memory with hypnosis."

"Is it working?"

"I think so," she admitted. "It's a process but it's better than sitting at home and doing nothing. I have to do what I can to stop this freak."

"Of course. Is there anything I can do?"

"Not unless you can tell me who did this to me," she quipped, a smidge of her former spunk returning.

"And what would you do to that person if I could?" he asked in a mildly playful tone. "Is it illegal?"

"Oh, absolutely," she said without a hint of hesitation. "I'm not even sure he'd survive."

"Bloodthirsty?"

"Only for his," she assured Chad with a small smile. "For what he did to me and Sierra…death would be a blessing after I was finished with him."

He chuckled and shoved the last bite of his sandwich

in his mouth. "You know—" he canted his gaze at her "—I believe you. I don't see fear in your eyes right now."

"Oh, yeah? What do you see?"

"I see rage."

Rage…yes, that was fair. And it felt good to admit it.

Sundance knocked on Iris's front door, carrying a pizza. He wasn't sure what he was doing, he just knew he wanted to spend the evening with her. After leaving Mya earlier that afternoon, he was a mess the rest of the day. His thoughts wouldn't stay focused, his train of thought was wrecked. He chalked it up to concern for Iris but he was kidding himself. He was more than concerned, he was agitated to the point of irrationality at the thought of Iris chatting it up with Chad.

Iris opened the door, Saaski at her side, and she smiled quizzically at his appearance. "You lost?"

"I thought you might be hungry and tired of casserole," he said, hefting the pepperoni pie. "How about it?"

"I've never been able to deny a man holding a pizza," she said, allowing him entry. He could feel her eyes on him and he didn't blame her. He was acting out of character. He set the pizza box down and she handed him a plate that he promptly filled with two healthy pieces. She balked at the size of the slices. "I'm not sure I can eat—"

"You can try. You've lost too much weight. And according to Mya, so have I. We are on strict orders to pig out with carte blanche."

She laughed, the sound warming him faster than a

hot toddy. "Well, Mya is a doctor. I suppose she knows what she's talking about."

"That's what I figured and there are worse pre-scriptions, right?"

"True." She accepted the plate and they walked into the living room, both sinking into the leather sofa. Sundance took a fat bite, eager to fill his mouth with something other than the awkward conversation threatening to fall from his lips. He and Iris had never had much in common—aside from their aversion to one another—and he didn't know how to engage her on a personal level. So he stuffed another bite in his mouth.

She, on the other hand, picked at the toppings, obviously not as hungry as he was.

"What's wrong?" he asked.

She shrugged. "Rough day."

Wiping his mouth, he swallowed and gave her his full attention. "How so?" She didn't want to talk about it, he could tell. He wanted her to feel secure with him, to at least trust him enough to share what she was going through. But he wasn't sure he had the right to be that person for her. He'd never been in this position before and he felt tongue-tied, unable to find the right thing to say. "I want to know," he said, trying to be encouraging.

"I'm fine."

"I'm beginning to hate that word," he grumbled, taking another bite and finishing his slice. "Just tell me."

"I don't want to," she grumbled back, flashing him a dark look. "It's nothing."

Was it something she could talk to Chad about? The

uncharitable thought shamed him but it didn't stop the chafing. "I want to help," he said.

She stopped plucking at her pepperoni and sighed unhappily. "There's nothing for you to do. This is something I have to do on my own. I have to be able to talk to men without flinching, without becoming overwhelmed with panic. Not everyone is out to get me but when the fear overcomes me, I can't think rationally."

"What happened?" he asked quietly.

"Chad Brown happened," she answered, disgust in her voice. "I freaked out over a simple statement."

"What did he say to upset you?" Sundance asked, trying hard to keep the growl from his voice. "I could have a talk with him."

"No, please don't. I already feel like I'm damaged. I don't need to confirm it to other people. It was an innocent statement that he made, but immediately I felt a chill wash over me and I couldn't breathe." Tears appeared in her eyes and their sudden appearance seemed to annoy her. She scrubbed at her eyes with agitation. "See? I can't even talk about it without crying. I'm a mess. Maybe I shouldn't even be working with patients yet. I can't continue to break down at the drop of a hat. Mya needs me to be like I was. *I* need me to be like I was." She stared at the moisture on her hand. "Instead, I'm this weak, pathetic victim who cries like a baby when the wind blows."

"You're no weakling," he assured her, shocked that she'd even think that about herself. "You're a woman to reckon with. You're a fighter, not a quitter." *It's what I love about you.* He wished he had the nerve to actually tell her. If anyone was weak, it was him.

"If I'm so strong, how come I still can't sleep through the night? I wake with night terrors, fighting and clawing at invisible hands, terrified that he's out there, waiting and watching me. Some pillar of strength, huh?"

He didn't hesitate, he gently drew Iris into his arms, where she went willingly, sinking into his embrace like someone who'd finally found safe harbor. It felt right to hold her like this and he wondered why he'd never realized before how much she meant to him. Knowing she was suffering so deeply, cut him and he'd do anything to ease her pain. "Don't confuse fear with cowardice. You are facing that fear every day like a warrior going into battle," he told her, smoothing her hair with slow, soothing strokes. "You are going to find your core again and you'll be stronger than ever before. I know you, Iris. And it's impossible for you to remain timid and scared. It's not in your nature. It never has been, not even when you were faced with terrible odds."

She sniffed against his chest and rubbed her nose. They remained that way for a long time, each lost in individual thoughts and memories. He would've given any amount of money to sneak a peek into her mind so he'd know how to comfort her.

Pulling away, she stared at him with red-rimmed eyes. "You don't have to do this," she said. "I don't like feeling like I'm an obligation. It's bad enough that I feel broken inside and you treating me with kid gloves just accentuates that fact."

She thought he was doing this out of obligation? He'd never understand the female mind. There was only one way he could imagine that would chase that thought away. Leaning down, he placed a gentle but firm kiss on her plump mouth. Her sharp intake of breath caused him to still, afraid he'd scared her, but when she met him for a second round, he knew it was okay. "Did that feel like obligation?" he asked huskily, his heart rate kicking a healthy staccato.

Iris swallowed and shook her head. "No," she whispered.

"All right then."

Chapter 19

He hadn't set out to become a serial rapist but life had a way of happening to people and before he knew it, he had a compulsion and a rather unfortunate label.

But he was never one to focus on the things he couldn't change. He was a doer, not a dweller.

And right now, something had to be done about Iris Beaudoin.

The thing was, Iris was breaking the rules and he couldn't have that. He hadn't built a significant portfolio of success to have it topple like a deck of cards under a stiff wind because one stubborn, bullheaded woman got it into her head to become a champion for all the poor, victimized women.

He'd been amused to see her struggle to find herself again. Her pain had tasted like fine chocolate; he'd wanted to savor every last moment, drink every salty tear.

But she was trying to put herself back together again and—bravo for chutzpah—but in her mission to become whole she was on a course to discover his identity.

And that was something that he couldn't let happen.

He imagined the fallout and it wasn't pretty.

No, his life would be ruined.

That left him with one recourse and he was loath to do it, for he truly wasn't a sadist—well, maybe just a little—but as he said, he was a doer and *something* had to be done about Iris Beaudoin.

Was it bad that he was going to enjoy it?

His mouth twisted in the tiniest of cruel smiles.

Yeah…a bit. But that's what made what he did so irresistible, so impossible to stop.

Hell, everyone had their vices, right?

A low chuckle rumbled from his chest as he faded into the night, the light from Iris's bedroom window shining like a beacon, bringing him home.

Iris awoke and turned to Sundance who lay on the bed with her, his chest rising and falling with the soft, even cadence of a man fast asleep and she wondered at the chain of events that had put this magnificent man in her bed.

He'd remained fully clothed, only kicking off his shoes to climb into the bed with her, drawing her close because she'd begun to shake uncontrollably. Somehow she'd fallen asleep, though she wasn't sure how it'd happened. As tightly wound as she'd been, she was fairly certain sleep wouldn't find her until the wee hours of the morning, but there was something about the feel of Sundance's arms around her that soothed her like a child and she'd drifted off easily.

A dark curtain of thick, long lashes—she used to tease him about them when they were younger because secretly she'd been ridiculously jealous—rested above proud, strong cheekbones. Really, he had the bone structure of a model but there was nothing soft or metrosexual about him. When they were kids she'd found his unrelenting stoicism annoying. Criminy, he was as stiff as hard oak. But right now, she appreciated his strength for she felt she had little to spare.

His lids flipped open, and she found herself staring into a set of eyes belonging to the man she'd longed for. It seemed unbearably cruel that it took something catastrophic for him to see her as a woman and equally unfair that now that he had, she felt unworthy of his attention.

"Did you sleep okay?" he asked, his voice scratchy from sleep.

She nodded shyly. "Best in weeks. You?"

He smiled. "What matters is that you slept well."

"I snore, don't I?" she asked fretfully, hating the idea that she'd kept him awake while she'd slept like the dead. "I'm sorry…"

He grinned. "You don't snore. But you do make a funny little breathy sound that is…odd. And mildly endearing," he said, when she'd begun to frown. He smoothed the skin between her brows with a light touch. "It's fine. I didn't sleep well because I'm still clothed. I've always slept—"

"—nude," she supplied, her cheeks coloring a bit. "I remember." Once when they were teens, she'd caught a glimpse of his bare backside when she'd sneaked in his room to grab an extra blanket. At the time she'd been horrified and terribly embarrassed. He'd yelled at her as he'd jerked the covers over his bare behind. She'd run from the room, dying from mortification. Mya had found it hilarious.

Sundance remembered, too, saying, "You should always knock before walking into a teenage boy's bedroom. You never know what they might be doing."

"I was just looking for an extra blanket," she retorted, her cheeks flaming, though a giggle wasn't far behind as she remembered the scene. "Besides, Mya was the one who sent me in there."

"Ah, and all these years I thought you were just trying to catch me naked."

"Hardly. If you recall, I didn't think much of you back in those days."

"I remember." He tucked strands of her thick hair behind her ear with a gentle touch. "And what do you think of me now?"

Her mouth played with a smile. "I think that's fairly obvious. Don't you think?"

He sobered and shook his head. "Nothing about a woman is obvious."

"Let me help you out then," she said, moving closer, cuddling into him, soaking up his warmth and enjoying the unique scent of his body. "I like this very much," she whispered, burying her nose against his chest. She smiled as his arms folded around her, holding her close.

She liked how he touched her reverently, as if she were some rare treasure. She would've never expected him to be so gentle. Everything about Sundance was hard, except his touch with her. She needed that so badly. Moisture pricked her eyes. She managed to hold back the tears but Sundance had noted the subtle tensing in her body and pulled away to regard the source.

"Was it something I did?" he asked, worried.

"No. Yes. Sort of," she amended, no doubt cementing his earlier sentiment about women being confusing. She rubbed at her nose. "Everything about me has changed. I no longer trust my instincts. I question my feelings. I don't know how to act around a man, much less one I'm attracted to, and being here with you is excruciating yet I don't want to give it up." He made a move as if to climb out of the bed, but she stopped him. "No, wait, please," she pleaded, hoping she could make sense of her own contradictions. He stilled, waiting for her to continue, his dark eyes intense and unfathomably dark. "I want you here, selfishly. You deserve a woman who isn't an emotional wreck. I break into tears at the slightest provocation, I'm paranoid over the smallest things, and I feel sick to my stomach at the idea of being intimate with someone. How is that fair to you?"

"Tears don't bother me, you've always been a little left-to-center about certain things, and as far as the intimacy goes, let's play it by ear. I'm not going anywhere unless you want me to. I'm willing to wait until you're ready."

Couldn't he see that she was trying to warn him? She ground the moisture from her eyes and glared. "Stop being so damn reasonable," she said, not surprised when her comment made him frown. "This isn't something that's easily fixed. I'm broken inside. Don't you get that? I can't promise you that I'll be fixed or get better ever. I can't live with that burden, why should I expect you to?"

He shrugged and climbed from the bed. "You need coffee. Let's figure everything else later. We could spend all morning arguing the points you've made but we both have work, so I say let's table this discussion until later."

She made a sound of exasperation but deep inside a curl of warmth teased her frosted insides, reminding her that she was dealing with a man nearly as stubborn as herself. He left the room and she heard him talking to Saaski, before the front door opened and closed. She smiled in spite of herself. He had made an excellent point. She didn't have time to convince him that he was wasting his energy on her because she needed to put her butt in gear. Mya was likely already on her way to the clinic—she always made a habit of getting there an hour early so she could ease into the caseload on her own schedule—and Iris liked to share a cup of coffee with her friend before the day started. Damn him, for knowing her schedule so well.

Iris slid from the bed and went in search of that coffee he'd been talking about and tried not to let her enjoyment of the moment between them sink too deeply into her bones.

She'd meant what she'd said and if he was smart, he'd take her words at face value. There was nothing subtle about what Iris was dealing with, and she'd never ask him to wait for her to figure it out because she knew all too well that it could take longer than they had years to live.

For not sleeping well, Sundance felt surprisingly refreshed. It probably wouldn't last but as long as he had a clear head, he was going to dig into the case again as soon as he got to the station.

He'd let Saaski out to relieve himself and run off some of that coiled energy housed in the big dog and then he'd set the coffee to percolating. He liked that Iris used an old-fashioned coffeepot rather than the automated ones with all the buttons and gadgets that took a degree in engineering to figure out. Plus, he thought the flavor was better with the old-fashioned percolation but Mya said that was all in his head. Maybe, maybe not.

He heard the shower start and busied himself with throwing together quick breakfast for them both. If Mya had been concerned over his weight, he was equally concerned that Iris was fading away before his eyes. Her lush curves had always been the stuff of men's dreams but he could see her collarbone sticking out, illuminating just how the strain of recent events had affected her. Normally, Iris had the appetite of a teenage boy. She could put away a surprising amount of food without blinking an eye. He knew because once he'd foolishly bet he could eat more pizza than her. She'd out-eaten him by two slices.

He'd just buttered the toast when the sound of glass shattering had him bolting for Iris's bathroom. He found her wrapped in a towel staring at the mirror above the sink, a broken water glass lying in shards on the tiled floor. The steam curled in the small room like a sauna, and all color leached from her face. He followed her stricken gaze and started when he saw the words that had appeared in the mirror with the help of the steam.

You were the best…

Iris backed away, her hand at her throat as she found her voice. "He was in my house," she said, sounding strangled and small. "Oh, my God."

"Don't touch anything," he instructed her, rage at the invasion kept at bay by the thinnest barrier. He had a camera in the Durango. First, he had to photograph the evidence, then he had to call in some help from the neighboring, larger reservation. He needed to collect forensic evidence, dust for prints, but he didn't have that kind of capability with his piddly resources. Iris's whole body was shaking and her lips moved soundlessly. She was going into shock. He reacted quickly, drawing her away from the bathroom, mindful of her bare feet and the glass. "Iris," he said gently but she was frozen, locked in fear. "Iris," he tried more firmly. She turned to stare at him, her eyes glazed. "I need you to get dressed but I need you to grab only what you absolutely need. I'm going to call in additional resources and find if he left anything else behind."

"I—I'm afraid," she stammered, tears sliding down her cheeks. "He was in my house. H-he might've been watching me in my sleep."

"I'm fairly certain he was not in the house when you were. Saaski would've eaten him alive. Chances are he gained access while you were at work because Saaski goes with you to the clinic. He must've known this."

At that Iris crumpled and would've slid to the floor if he hadn't caught her. She sobbed into her hands, barely coherent. "Why is he doing this to me? Isn't it enough he ruined my life? What kind of sadistic bastard is he to violate me twice?"

Sundance didn't know, but he had a feeling, whoever had done this had just changed his MO.

Iris watched as law enforcement strangers from the neighboring tribe came to help gather forensic evidence for Sundance. She'd managed to get the shakes under control but inside she felt her core had turned to ice. She couldn't quite get warm enough no matter how many layers of clothing she had on. Sundance had called Mya to let her know what was going on, and true to form, Mya had driven like a madwoman over to the house as soon as her replacement had been called in.

Mya held Iris's hand, rubbing the numb flesh. "You're

like a Popsicle," she admonished, looking to Sundance for help, but he was preoccupied with the evidence collection. In fact, he fairly prowled the small house like a caged beast, his frustration evident with every step. "Tell me exactly what happened," Mya instructed, her voice warm but worried.

"I'd gotten out of the shower and went to brush my teeth when I saw the words in the mirror because of the steam. He knew they'd show up and I'd see it. This is a deliberate attempt to get my attention and it worked," she said, a note of hysteria creeping into her voice until she choked it down. "I don't know what I'm going to do. I don't feel safe at all. What does he want?"

"I don't know," Mya said sorrowfully. "But I think you're right, you're not safe here anymore. Maybe you should come stay with me until we get this figured out."

"And put you in harm's way?" Iris shook her head vehemently. "No. I can't do that. This man is a monster… worse than I imagined." Her eyes widened as a separate thought came to her. "Oh, no, someone needs to warn James. If he found a way to sneak into my home, he might do it to Sierra, too."

"Sundance will take care of it," Mya assured her. "If he hasn't already. We need to focus on you right now. This man is fixating on you and I won't let you stay here by yourself. Please come stay with me."

"I can't," Iris said, shuddering at the thought of bringing that maniac into her best friend's life. She would never willingly put Mya in danger, not even to save herself. She gripped Mya's hand and forced a brave smile. "I'll figure something out," she promised, but Mya wasn't convinced and tried a different tack.

"Then stay with Sonny," she suggested. "I know he wouldn't mind."

It was probably the safest route but she hated being chased from her home and her bitterness leached out in her voice. "I can't just invite myself into Sundance's space like a Motel 6. He didn't sign up for a houseguest."

"Stop," Mya said, her voice soft but firm. "You know he cares about you. Let him help you. Besides, offering a friend a bed for a few nights is not exactly going to turn his life upside down. If you won't stay with me, promise me you'll stay with Sonny. I won't rest unless I know you're safe."

"Mya…" But her friend wouldn't be swayed and Iris could tell by the pinched set of her mouth that she was going to dig in her heels, and if it came down to it, Mya would drag her from this house and hog-tie her for her own good. She sighed and nodded, finally conceding. "I'll ask him."

Mya's relief was immediate. "Thank you. Has anyone ever told you how damn stubborn you are?" she asked with mock severity. Mya rubbed at her eyes, watching as the team went to and from the bedroom carrying plastic bags of possible evidence while another took pictures of the point of entry, that happened to be the back door where the lock was flimsy. It was something Sundance had been after Iris to change since she inherited the house from her mother nearly five years ago.

Saaski, uncomfortable with all the strange sights and smells, remained stationed at Iris's feet, a low rumble deep in his chest when someone happened to get too close. On autopilot Iris reached down to give the big dog's head a good, soothing scratch so he would settle.

"One thing is for sure, that dog isn't going to let anyone get near you," Mya said.

Iris smiled, grateful. "Yes, that's the one thing that's keeping me sane. If I thought this sick freak had somehow gotten into my house while I slept, I'd lose my mind. But I know Saaski would never let that happen. I think Sundance is right, whoever came into my house did it when I was at work."

"I think it's also someone who knows you and possibly lives on the reservation," Mya said in a hushed tone. "Which I don't have to tell you, gives me the creeps."

Iris managed a wry twist of her lips. "Yeah, I know. The question is, who?"

Mya shuddered. "I don't know but I hope Sundance figures it out soon. I don't like this. I have a feeling something bad is coming if he doesn't."

Iris wished Mya hadn't voiced aloud what she was already dreading. But it was out there, just like the person who'd done this.

Chapter 20

"I think that about does it."

Sundance stopped what he was doing to shake the hand of the man responsible for the swift response to his call out. Russell "Barking Dog" Jacy was head of the forensic team in the neighboring Quinault Nation. They had more resources than Sundance and he wasn't above asking for help, especially when it seemed the stakes had just been upped.

Russell shook his head, something causing him to frown. "You know, I heard about the attacks that happened here and I couldn't help but think that it seems similar to what happened on our reservation about two years ago."

"Did you catch who was responsible?"

"No. The case went cold and it's been quiet ever since."

"How many victims?" Sundance asked.

"Three, that we know of. Sometimes these types of crimes aren't reported so we're not sure if there were more."

Of course, Sundance's reservation was considerably smaller than that of the Quinault Nation. It would be damn near impossible to hide that kind of thing here; however, on a bigger rez, it might go unreported just like Russell said. "The victims, were they drugged?"

"Yeah, ketamine. Not the usual drug of choice anymore for date rapers from what I hear because of the high incidence of death. Whoever is doing this must have some kind of knowledge about the drug to use it so skillfully. We'd done a search of the area vets but everyone came up clean. After that we just plain ran out of leads to follow."

"Why the vets?" he asked, snagging on the odd detail.

"Because vets often use ketamine for anesthesia. They have the easiest access to it."

Sundance digested the information, his mind going arrow-straight to Paul Brown but he kept quiet for the time being. He couldn't very well start voicing suspicions about a top level BIA employee without ruffling feathers.

"Not so skillfully," Sundance said. "He nearly killed the sixteen-year-old girl he drugged. It was only because her boyfriend found her and raced her to the urgent care center that she didn't die."

"That's rough for a kid to go through. All our vics were in their mid- to late-twenties, all single ladies, too."

A random thought came to Sundance. "When you were investigating your cases did you contact the neighboring tribes to see if there were any similar cases?"

"No, we didn't," Russell said, frowning as if trying to remember details. "Honestly, the attacks stopped as abruptly as they started. We were just happy to see them end and the victims weren't interested in rehashing the event over again so when the trail went cold…"

"You let it go," Sundance finished for him. Russell seemed chagrined to admit this but Sundance wasn't interested in passing judgment. "I have a theory that whoever is doing this has been doing it for a while. I'll bet if we dig a little harder, we'll find more victims assaulted with the same MO."

"Sounds plausible," Russell said, a seemingly permanent crease deepening in his forehead. "I'll make some calls and let you know if anything comes up."

"You're a good man," Sundance said, gripping Russell's hand.

Russell packed up and headed out with the rest of the team he'd brought from the Quinault Nation. Sundance found Mya and Iris deep in conversation, talking about something that clearly made Iris agitated. He approached and they both looked up. "They found a few partial prints that might yield something and bagged a few things they think might've been handled by the intruder, and they're putting a rush on the forensics due to the possibility that there are multi-jurisdictional cases involved here. Still, I suspect we won't hear anything until the end of the week, one way or another."

"That long?" Mya asked, distressed. "That seems like an eternity to sit here and wait."

He agreed but there was little anyone could do about that. He'd rather focus on what he could change, rather than bang his head against a cedar. "In the meantime, I don't want you staying here," he announced.

Iris and Mya shared a glance and he realized they

must've already broached this subject. Iris exhaled and squared her shoulders, nodding. "Mya offered her place—"

"I'm not comfortable with that," he cut in, earning a stubborn look from Iris but he wasn't going to budge on this. There was only one place he'd agree to and that was his place. "Mya isn't in a position to protect you if this person comes looking for you. She doesn't carry a gun and isn't trained to use one. No, the best place is with me."

Mya smiled, knowing full well he'd say that, and simply kissed Iris on the cheek, saying, "You're in good hands. Take care, love."

Iris watched Mya leave and Sundance said, "You'd already made the decision to go home with me, hadn't you?"

"Yeah, Mya is as stubborn as the both of us when she really sets her mind to something. You don't mind do you? I could sleep on the couch."

"I wouldn't offer if I didn't mean it. I'm going to do a perimeter check and while I'm doing that why don't you gather an overnight bag. Grab some dog food for Saaski, too." He didn't wait for her to agree or chatter, he wanted to get Iris out of the house. It felt contaminated to him, knowing that her home had been invaded. He hated this helpless feeling, it ate at him like a cancer. If he didn't find a way to solve this case it might put him in an early grave.

Iris had always secretly loved Sundance's house. He'd built it on the land inherited through his family but instead of making do with the old house, he'd razed it to the ground and built fresh, putting blood and sweat into the equity.

The modest house was simple yet classic with its strong lines and sturdy craftsmanship. Saaski sniffed at the unfamiliar surroundings like a sentinel at duty, prowling the confines of the house until he felt satisfied nothing was lurking in the shadows that he could bite or eat. He settled by the woodstove as Sundance made quick work of stoking the embers to blaze again with fresh wood.

"Are you hungry?" he asked, moving to the open kitchen. "Damn, I should've had you bring one of those casseroles."

"I'm casseroled out," she declared, though she felt somehow guilty for saying it. Mya had gone to a lot of trouble to make those casseroles for her and she felt obligated to eat every damn one of them. "I'm not really hungry," she said. "Just a bit thirsty."

"Juice okay? I don't have alcohol."

She smiled. "Juice sounds great." It would likely be a long time before she could stomach alcohol again after what she'd been through.

Was it weird that she was sitting in Sundance's living room watching as he went about something so domestic as getting her a glass of apple juice? Hell, yes. But she'd be a liar if she didn't admit to finding it soothing, too.

Sundance returned with a glass of juice and a water for himself. He settled onto the sofa, looking worn. She inched toward him, not quite sure of her place in his life and afraid of overstepping. When he seemed open to her approach, she nestled into the crook of his arm, draping her arm across his chest. The muted sound of the logs crackling behind the closed woodstove door made everything seem cozy and safe. Tucked against Sundance, she almost fooled herself into thinking all things were possible, including a true relationship with him, but even as she cleaved to the comforting thought, something dark and menacing hovered at the edges of her happiness, the knowledge that someone was out there, waiting to hurt her again.

She squeezed her eyes shut as if that alone could prevent it from happening.

Sundance tightened his hold on her, conveying without words that he felt her fear and met it head-on with his strength even though she knew the mental stress was wearing him down.

"If we don't find this person, you ought to consider leaving the reservation," he said, his voice heavy. She startled and lifted her head to stare at him. He wore the weight of the world on his shoulders and every pound seemed etched in his eyes. He ran a knuckle down her cheek. "If I can't keep you safe I want you as far away from this place as you can go."

"I won't leave," she said. "I won't let him take my family from me, as well. I'll get a gun if I have to. If he tries to hurt me again I'll blow him all over creation."

He smiled as if he liked the idea of that but it didn't last. "He isn't likely to just show up on your doorstep. He's a sneaky bastard. He'll try and catch you unaware, that's his signature. He doesn't want someone in a fair fight. He wants to make sure the odds are always in his favor, which means even if you had a gun, you might not be able to get to it when you need to."

"That's what Saaski is for," she maintained stubbornly. "I know he'd break a few bones if he sensed I was in danger."

"Yes, I know he would but there are so many variables," he said on a sigh. "I hate the idea of you being in danger. It makes me sick to my stomach. It's like fighting an invisible opponent. You never know when they're going to strike and they could be standing right in front of you but you'd never know."

Iris understood his frustration but she couldn't let some psycho rule her life. She bit back her protests, knowing they would only serve to worry Sundance more and she wouldn't do that for the world. He was already taking on so much, she wouldn't dream of adding to his burden.

They remained quiet for a long while, both too tired to do much else than simply enjoy the silence but Iris couldn't keep one thing from poking at her.

"Why have things changed between us? Is it because of the attack?" she asked.

He stilled and she almost told him to forget it, she didn't want to know but that'd be a lie because she needed to know. If his feelings were grounded in the fact that she'd been victimized and he felt responsible, she couldn't trust what was happening between them.

"It's late, we should get to bed," he said, pulling away. He held his hand out to her and she accepted it, though her heart was sad. He wasn't answering her question. His deflection was answer enough. "You're welcome to sleep with me or if you're more comfortable on the couch I'll get you some blankets and a pillow."

She ought to sleep on the couch. But it would be hard enough to sleep in unfamiliar surroundings much less after the day she'd had.

Iris tried to keep her heartache from her smile as she said, "I want to sleep beside you, Sundance."

His eyes warmed for the briefest moment and he tucked her into his side as they walked into the bedroom.

* * *

The next few weeks passed in a strange twilight zone of domestic bliss for Iris. She and Sundance went home together, ate dinner, chatted about their day, did their individual tasks and then, at the end of the night, retired together. Iris had quickly become accustomed to the comforting bulk of Sundance's warm body pressed against hers and the fact that he never tried to push her boundaries, only served to endear him to her even more. He had the patience of a saint. She'd never known the depth of his restraint until the night he'd bounded from the bed, terrified he'd scare her when he'd inadvertently gotten an erection.

Bless him, she'd tried not to laugh because his concern was grounded in reality. She hadn't yet been able to contemplate the idea of sex, even with Sundance whom she was fairly certain she was falling in love with, but when he'd leaped from the bed like a superhero avoiding the one thing that could kill him, something inside of her had melted.

"Come back to bed," she said in a husky murmur, smiling when he'd shook his head in agitation. "Come on—" she patted the bed in invitation "—it's okay."

"I'm sorry," he ground out, clearly annoyed with himself, pushing a hand through his hair. "It's difficult being so close to you and knowing I can't touch you."

"You can touch me," she whispered on a nod.

"Are you sure?" he asked.

"Yes."

He hesitated, the conflict written plainly across the planes of his face, but he slid back into the bed and gathered her close with a gentle touch. She closed her eyes, quelling the panic when his erection nudged her bare thigh, reminding herself with the scent and touch of the man she cared for deeply, that Sundance would never force her, that he wasn't the man who'd hurt her.

"You're trembling," he noted, distress in his voice.

She clutched him tighter. "I know."

He pressed a kiss to her crown, his arms closing around her like a cocoon of warmth and safety, and he murmured, "Whenever you're ready, sweetheart. I'm willing to wait."

And just like that, any doubt she might've had about her feelings fled like a bad dream in the morning light.

He might not know what his feelings were but she knew where hers were living and breathing and for the moment, that was enough to sustain her.

It was late afternoon on a Sunday, the chatter on the dispatch radio had been subdued, likely due to the sheets of rain that drenched the land causing everyone to hunker down in their homes to wait it out, and Sundance was savoring the day spent being lazy with Iris.

She sat curled on the sofa, her feet tucked up under her while she read a book. She'd put her hair up in a messy knot at the back of her head, and the stray strands that escaped the hair band trailed down her back. She wore her reading glasses, something she'd reluctantly brought from her place when he realized she'd been trying to make do without them, and he wondered how he'd ever been so blind.

It was hard to remember thinking that she was funny-looking.

She glanced up and caught him staring. A shy blush colored her cheeks as if she knew the bent of his thoughts—of the hunger that tightened on his insides—

and he longed to take her into his arms and feel those beautiful, full breasts pressed against his chest.

"Is there something wrong?" she asked, lowering her book to peer at him with worry.

He shook his head and closed the distance between them, her delightfully surprised smile warming him to his toes. She removed her glasses in a self-conscious movement and he chuckled at her vanity. "You'd be beautiful covered in mud," he assured her softly. "I can't believe I ever thought you were ugly."

She gasped in mock offense. "Ugly?"

He grinned, reaching up to twine a lock of hair on his finger. "Yeah, don't you remember I used to call you fish lips?"

Iris's laughter filled him with joy. "I do. But I thought you were just being mean."

"Oh, I was, but there was some truth to it, too, at least I thought so at the time. Of course, now I realize I was an idiot."

"I believe you also used to call me boulder boobs," she recalled.

At the mention of her breasts, his groin heated. He managed a chuckle. "Yeah. Again, I was an idiot."

She put her book down and wrapped her arms around him. "So now that you're newly enlightened, what do you want to call me?"

Mine. The simple word sprang to his lips but he held it back. She leaned forward and pressed a featherlight kiss to his temple, murmuring, "No more fish lips?"

"No," he answered huskily, burying his face in the soft skin at her neck, nuzzling the junction where her neck met her shoulders. "Sweetness, perfection, hot as hell," he growled, wishing he could lay her down and show her how much she meant to him, but knew it still wasn't time to go that far. He pulled back with effort and met her soft gaze. "Am I forgiven?"

She made a show of considering his request, then said playfully, "How about we're even?"

"Even?"

"Well, do you remember having a giant crush on Karen Reynolds in school?" she asked.

He nodded. "Yeah," he answered, wondering where she was going with this. Karen had been a year below him in school but three years ahead of Iris and Mya. He'd been certain she liked him, too, until one day she'd started avoiding him. It'd been a serious blow to his high school ego. "What about it?"

She giggled. "Well, I might've had something to do with her sudden decision to date Bryan Strather instead."

He sat up, regarding her with the same mock offense. "What?"

"Yeah...I might've let it slip in conversation after gym class that you..."

"That I what?" He started a slow climb up her body, loving her delighted shriek and playful protests. She wrapped her arms and legs around him and he claimed her mouth. She accepted his tongue, tentatively tangling with his, slowly regaining her confidence. He retreated, staring into her dark eyes, drinking in how lucky he was to be with her. She touched his cheek with her knuckle. He raised an eyebrow. "Out with it, Beaudoin," he instructed softly. "Or face the consequences."

She bit her lip in an endearingly sexy manner as she said, "Well, I may have told her that you were a...bed wetter."

His eyes widened and Karen's distaste when he'd asked her to the winter homecoming flashed in his memory. "Why, you little devil," he exclaimed, raising her shirt to tickle her stomach with the scruff on his chin. "Payback is coming, sweet cheeks. Payback is coming!"

They rolled onto the floor and he cushioned their fall with his body so that she landed on top. As she stared down at him, a smile playing on her generous lips and a sparkle in her eyes, he was consumed with the overwhelming desire to shelter her from any harm. He'd give his life for hers.

Of that he was certain.

Thoughts buzzed around the darkness that threatened her—the knowledge that a serial rapist was likely biding his time for the right moment to strike—but he pushed them away. He needed this. She needed it, too.

It was selfish, but right now, he just wanted to enjoy the simple pleasure of being with her.

Chapter 21

Iris took her lunch to her favorite spot on the terrace. The weather was "abominable" as Mya put it, but Iris never minded the dark rain clouds, not even before her attack when her outlook on life had been considerably rosier. She munched on the sandwich Sundance had packed for her, smiling on the inside for his careful consideration for her welfare. He hadn't made a big production about it, just handed her a sack filled with goodies. She'd accepted it with a grin and rewarded him with a kiss.

She'd only just finished her sandwich when she realized she wasn't alone. She jumped instinctively, her hand flying to her throat as if to hold back her heart from leaping out of her body, until she realized it was Sierra's father, James.

"Sorry to bother you, Iris, but I need to talk to you for a minute," he said.

"Of course, what's wrong? Is it Sierra?" she asked, not surprised when he nodded miserably. "Tell me what's happening."

"She won't talk to no one but she screams at night in her sleep." Iris swallowed the last bite that felt stuck in her throat. She knew exactly what the teen was going through except she had Sundance and Sierra had no one but her father. "I don't know what to do. Could you talk to her? Maybe if you talk to her she might snap out of it and get back to living."

"I'd be happy to talk to Sierra," she murmured but she wouldn't give him false hope. There was a chance Sierra would never be the girl he remembered. Heaven knew she wasn't the same. A thought came to her. "Do you think she'd be open to hypnosis?"

James frowned, not liking the idea but desperate. "Will it help?"

"I don't know. It's helping me. It's worth a try, right?" she said.

"I suppose. Will you go with her? I don't like the idea of her going alone."

"Of course. You can come, too, if that would make you more comfortable. Dr. Seryn is the nicest person I've ever met, aside from Mya. She's very gentle."

James shook his head. "No, you can take her. My truck's not so reliable these days and I think it'd just be best if you took her."

Iris understood what James wasn't saying. He felt out of his element but he wouldn't stand in the way of his daughter getting help. "Let me set it up and I'll call you with the time."

"Thank you," he said, his eyes filling with tears. "She's all I got. It's breaking me into pieces to see her so changed. She's not my little butterfly girl any longer. I want her back."

Hot tears filled her eyes but she held them back for James's sake. "Okay. I'll help in any way I can."

Sundance received a call from Russell and the news wasn't good.

"No matches on any of the prints we managed to get, aside from yours and Iris's. Sorry, man. I really hoped something would match up."

Sundance swore softly. "Did you get any hits on the calls to neighboring tribes?" he asked, hoping for at least something to go their way.

"Not exactly but I did hit on something. I'm not sure it matches your case, though. The MO is similar but the hit came from an Oregon tribe, near to the Washington border."

"What are the details?"

"A handful of girls drugged and raped, some with ketamine in their system. None remembered their attacker and the cases went cold for lack of evidence. Even though it's another state, I gotta tell you, the hairs on my neck stood straight up when I read this. Of course, back then DNA analysis and collection wasn't what it is today. Anything that might've been usable is long gone now."

"This person is following American-Indian tribes… somehow he's associated with the reservations he's hitting." Sundance thought for a long moment, his brain working fast. Paul Brown's name came to mind immediately. "Did you run the prints against all databases? Federal included?"

"No, just the criminal records."

"Try the federal database and include everyone ever fingerprinted to work within a sovereign nation."

"That search would take days," Russell stated incredulously. "Let's narrow the field a bit."

"Fine. Narrow it to the three surrounding states. Something tells me he has a home base that he doesn't stray too far from but the crimes are spread out enough to prevent suspicion."

"Give me a day. I'll see what I can come up with."

"Thanks," Sundance said, feeling for the first time in weeks as if their luck had changed.

Sierra, once a pretty and vivacious girl, sat across from Dr. Seryn, a shell of her former self.

A shell who didn't care about bathing, eating or interacting with people. And Iris saw herself before Sundance forced her to come to terms with life. Frankly, she'd been surprised Sierra had agreed to come to see Dr. Seryn.

Dr. Seryn took one look at Sierra and Iris knew the girl was in good hands. The good doctor wouldn't rest until Sierra had returned to the land of the living. She might never be the carefree butterfly girl again but at least she wouldn't be the zombie sitting across from them.

Iris went to wait outside while Sierra started her session but the girl latched on to her hand, her eyes pleading with her not to leave. She clasped Sierra's hand. "If you want me to stay I will. Nothing is going to hurt you here. Dr. Seryn is a wonderful doctor who knows what she's doing." Sierra's grip didn't loosen and Iris smiled to reassure her. "I'll stay."

"Thank you," Sierra mumbled, reluctantly letting go

of Iris's hand when she saw that she was indeed going to stay.

Iris sank into a chair away from Dr. Seryn and Sierra and hoped the girl was able to relax enough to gain some benefit from the session. Unlike Iris's sessions, that were geared toward identifying her attacker, Dr. Seryn's mission for Sierra was to heal the gaping wound inside her mind. Her body had healed but her psyche wept from giant fissures.

"Sierra, I want you to close your eyes and imagine a safe place, somewhere filled with joy and happiness, light and freedom. This can be a made-up place or some place from your childhood. Paint your landscape with bright and beautiful colors…"

Dr. Seryn's voice lulled Iris into a relaxed state even though she wasn't intending on participating. Cushioned with deep, fluffy pillows, Iris drifted into a dream that felt more real than illusion.

Laughter, music from the bar that night, and really bad singing filled her head.

Her heart felt light, her troubles far.

A familiar voice whispered in her ear and her good feelings drained away. Panic replaced happiness; fear overwrote joy.

A face—smiling from ear to ear with forced charm—loomed in her vision. She tried to back away but he remained in her face, leering.

She tried pushing, he only got closer.

Iris could smell cinnamon on his breath, could feel the heat of his body against hers. She scratched and clawed, though half the time her feeble swipes met with air and laughter. But she managed to connect with one good hit. The laughter turned to a howl of rage. Her body was buffeted by his fists but she felt no pain. The sound of her clothes tearing made her cry out; she knew what would come next.

She fought him but it was as if she were slogging through mud, her arms lacked strength and it was getting harder to breathe. His weight on top of her squeezed the air from her lungs. She smelled the sharp cologne, expensive maybe.

He grunted against her yet she felt nothing. It was as if her entire body were encased in numbing cream, preventing her nerve endings from firing properly, signaling that she was being brutalized from head to toe.

It was dark, and scary things slithered in and out of her vision. She squeezed her eyes shut but forced them open again, though it took a Herculean effort. His face was a grotesque mask, horrifying and unnatural. A scream rattled in her paralyzed throat and died without making it past her lips.

He finished and pushed off her.

"What do you see, baby?" he grunted in a guttural voice that surely couldn't be real as he buckled his pants. "It's the drugs. Wicked trip, huh? Don't worry, it'll wear off and you won't remember a thing."

Blood trickled down her throat but she could do nothing about it. She would die out here, choking on her own blood.

"Maybe if you're lucky, we'll do it again sometime. You're a hot piece of tail, that's for sure."

Footsteps retreated and she heard the sound of a car engine starting. Gravel spit under tires and he was gone.

She lay there a long time, or maybe it was minutes. She wasn't sure. She managed to slowly roll to her side so that the blood could seep onto the ground instead of down her throat.

Then she slid into darkness.

Iris's eyes popped open, wrenched free from the dream, and she grabbed frantically at the sides of the chair, her heart thundering.

Dr. Seryn paused with Sierra to regard Iris with concern. Iris sealed her mouth shut so she didn't start babbling like a hysterical child and scare Sierra. She needed to talk with Sundance—now!

Sundance dropped by Chad's office, wondering how to broach the subject that was most on his mind. He wasn't sure how to tell Chad his father had become a suspect in his investigation. He hoped he had Chad's cooperation but there was only one way to find out.

Except he wasn't given the opportunity, for not only was Brett Duncan's office cubicle cleaned out but Chad's office was dark and empty, as well.

He turned to someone stationed in another cubicle and asked, "Where's Duncan and the boss?"

The woman glanced up at Sundance, noted his badge and answered with a faint frown. "Well, Brett is no longer with us. He gave his notice today, and as far as the boss, he didn't say where he was going. I assumed he was taking a late lunch."

Sundance murmured his thanks for her help and wondered why Brett Duncan up and quit so suddenly. He knew the man had an alibi, but damn if he didn't want the guy for the crime. But seeing as he had nothing by the way of evidence, and being a cheating jerk wasn't enough cause to arrest someone, he could do little about him splitting the reservation. *Good riddance,* he thought, moving on.

Sundance thought about leaving Chad a message but decided against it, figuring he'd catch him tomorrow.

But as it turned out, it wasn't necessary since Chad rolled up in his government-issue sedan just as Sundance was climbing into the Durango.

"Hey, taking off so soon? I have promising news to share," Chad said, breaking into an easy grin. "I think I might've found a grant that will help funnel some much-needed cashola into this place. I think that deserves a dinner invitation, don't you?"

A leap of excitement caused his mouth to twitch into a grin. Was it possible? He'd given up on the hope of grant funds when they hadn't been able to find anyone with the experience to write up the proposals. If the grant was a possibility because of Brett Duncan, Sundance realized he'd have to eat a little crow. "How'd you find it?" he asked.

"Hey, it helps to have connections," Chad said, his eyes twinkling. "I've been working with reservations for the past fifteen years in various capacities. You pick up a few tips along the way and I was more than happy to put that experience to good use here."

"I thought maybe your father might've used some of his influence," Sundance said.

Chad's enthusiasm dampened and his mouth actually tightened with ill-disguised disgust before he let it go and said, "Naw, the old man doesn't give a crap about anyone but the people who can further his career. Actually, this one was all on me."

"What about your grant guy?"

"Yeah, I might've overestimated his talents. I let him go this morning. Sad, on paper he seemed the real deal but, I don't know, there was something about his personality that rubbed me the wrong way."

That was exactly how Sundance felt. "Can't say that I'll miss him," he admitted.

"Yeah, you and me both. I was tired of his whining about his marriage all the time. Blah, blah, blah… leave the bitch already," Chad said, laughing. "It's not like there isn't plenty of tail out there, just waiting for the right opportunity." Chad's statement struck an odd note with Sundance. Chad brightened, saying, "So what say you about that dinner? And how about setting me up with that growling fine sister of yours? Damn, she's hot enough to melt your eyeballs."

Sundance tried not to stiffen but he didn't like the way Chad was talking about Mya. It wasn't that he'd said anything truly offensive, but it didn't sit well with Sundance. He ignored Chad's hopeful request, deciding now was as good a time as any to address the real reason he'd come looking for the man.

"Listen, I've got to talk to you about something."

"Sounds serious."

"It is. It's about your dad."

Chad sighed. "Did he harass some poor woman? I'm always telling him to keep his hands to himself. He's pretty old-school about some things. I'll talk to him," he assured Sundance, assuming that was the problem.

"No, it's nothing like that."

"What is it then?"

"It's about the case."

Chad frowned. "What's the case got to do with my dad?"

"I need to ask him a few questions. All the victims, including ones in neighboring tribes were drugged with ketamine, that is a common drug used by veterinarians. The fact that your dad was once a vet and has had associations with every tribe reporting an unsolved rape case makes him suspect. I'm sorry."

Chad's mouth tightened and he shook his head. "This is career suicide, man. Don't do it. This sounds way too circumstantial to screw your career over. You start spouting off stuff like that and my dad will bury you. Trust me. And, honestly, I gotta tell you, this is some special kind of crap. I think you're grasping at straws because you're desperate. Frankly, I thought you were a better investigator than that."

Sundance had expected anger so Chad's defense of his father didn't offend him.

"So you must have new leads or something…" Chad surmised, then he said, "No, don't tell me. I don't need to know. Although I just wondered because Iris had mentioned she was doing hypnosis or something to try and remember details, though why she'd want to remember is beyond me."

"Every detail helps," Sundance said.

"I suppose…if hypnosis really worked. Most MDs consider it a bunch of hogwash."

"Well, it seems to be working," Sundance said, feeling the need to defend Iris's therapy, possibly because he'd been the one to suggest it for her. "Besides, she's seeing a forensic hypnotherapist, not your average run-of-the-mill practitioner."

Chad shrugged, the movement still resonating with anger. "Well, good luck. You're barking up the wrong tree but you're going to do what you feel is necessary. I just wish I'd known I was working with a loose cannon, willing to throw away months of hard work on a hunch. This isn't *Scooby-Doo* and there are real consequences for a monumental screwup."

Chad jerked his car door open and climbed inside without offering a goodbye.

Sundance gave him his space and watched him drive away. There was no good way to deliver bad news. He figured it went as well as could be expected. But he suspected Chad's warning held merit. If he was wrong, he was about to royally screw his future…and possibly that of the entire tribe.

Iris dropped Sierra off at home and drove like a crazy woman to the station. Her cell phone was dead and Sierra hadn't brought one; that left her unable to talk to anyone about what she'd seen while with Dr. Seryn.

She'd never expected her own brain to kick in with the memory overload but maybe that's what finally tripped the lock, she'd been completely relaxed and open when before she'd been tense and afraid.

Iris arrived at the station in a puff of dust, and when she saw that Sundance wasn't there she realized he must be out on a call. Well, she'd go to his place then and wait for him. She scribbled a note and tacked it to the front door for when Sundance returned and then headed for his place with one small detour. She'd left Saaski at home rather than take him to Dr. Seryn's with them since Sierra had been fearful of the big dog.

Iris pulled into her driveway, the small house pricking an odd note of sadness as it no longer felt welcoming to her. She shook off the melancholy, focused on grabbing a few essentials and Saaski, then heading out.

Saaski barked with happiness, his bushy tail wagging while his tongue lolled as he strained against his chain. Iris unhooked him and he bounded into the forest behind the house, presumably to work off the energy he had from being tied for a few hours. She smiled, knowing Saaśki would return if she whistled.

She headed into the house, going straight for her bedroom to grab fresh clothes. Finished, she plopped her bag on the sofa while she went to the kitchen to package up the rest of her casseroles. She pulled the first casserole from the freezer but nearly dropped it when she realized someone was standing in the doorway.

"I knocked but I guess you didn't hear me."

Iris's grip tightened on the casserole, her skin prickling as her heart rate sped up. "Chad…what are you doing here?" She didn't ask how he knew where she lived. She already knew. He knew because he'd been there before. His was the voice she recognized from her session with Dr. Seryn. She forced a smile. "Actually, you caught me just as I was leaving."

"That's a shame," Chad said, a charming smile looking the exact opposite to her as he approached. She went very still, but kept her fixed smile. He didn't know she knew. If she remained normal, he'd suspect nothing and she would be able to walk away. He gestured to the casserole. "What you got there?"

"Dinner. For me and Sundance."

"Sounds cozy."

"He's a good friend."

"Is that all?"

Iris's smile slipped. "What do you mean?"

"Oh, c'mon, Iris, don't play dumb. It's beneath you. I want to know if you let him between your legs or not."

Her hands had begun to shake. "Get out," she demanded, her voice thin and reedy.

Chad shook off the charming smile he'd been wearing and walked toward her with a lazy stride, as if he had all the time in the world because he knew they wouldn't be disturbed.

Sweat popped along her hairline and her fingers ached from gripping the pan so tightly. Panic fluttered at the edges of her sanity.

Chad tsked. "So rude. Where are your manners?" He sighed and slid on a pair of black gloves, the action freezing the marrow in her bones. Chad shook his head, chuckling. "It's okay. It's hard to be on your best behavior all the time. I can definitely relate."

Her eyes darted to the window facing her side yard, searching for Saaski but she couldn't see him. She returned to Chad who was watching her with cold, flat eyes. He flexed his fingers, showcasing the gloves. "Nice, huh? I had to ditch the latex. Made me itch. These are spy-quality. Found them in a specialty store in San Francisco. Guaranteed to leave behind no prints. That's important, as you can imagine."

"Why are you doing this?" she managed to whisper, though her tongue felt stuck to the roof of her mouth from fear.

"Why?" he repeated, frowning as if the question should be obvious. "Because you remember."

"I won't tell anyone," she promised, but he shook his head, annoyed.

"Don't waste your breath on stupid promises we both know you won't keep. Besides, think of how awkward things would be later when I start dating Mya. I think I might marry her, actually. But first, details."

She wanted to scream at him that Mya would never let him touch her but she knew not to agitate him further. The key was to keep him talking, perhaps to buy herself more time to figure out a solution. "Why me?"

Chad actually seemed pleased that she asked.

"Because you were special. All my girls are in some way but I knew *you'd* be the one to cause trouble. Even so I couldn't resist. What man with my tastes could? The thought of breaking you was too much to pass up. But in the end," he admitted wryly, "it's the one you should walk away from that causes you to make mistakes." He broke out into a grin. "Maybe I ought to have another taste…for old time's sake. What do you say?"

"G-go s-screw yourself," she stammered, the shake more pronounced as desperation set in. She wasn't going to let him touch her again. She thought of Sierra and every woman he'd defiled with his wicked cruelty and she choked down rising bile. She took in his tall, lean build and seemingly good looks and she knew how easy it must be for him to find victims, likely as easy as shooting fish in a barrel, and the resultant rage seared away the fear freezing her limbs. And he thought he'd defile her again? She'd rather die. She held the heavy casserole, waiting. The door was just a few feet beyond him. She could distract him and run.

It was her only chance. If she failed…she wouldn't leave this house alive.

She could read it in his eyes.

He was here to tie up loose ends.

Sundance couldn't shake the feeling that something was off. His instincts clanged like a bell when he couldn't reach Iris on her cell phone. He knew she'd gone with Sierra to see Dr. Seryn but they should've been back by now. He tried calming his nerves, rationalizing that it was likely Iris hadn't charged her phone and she was probably running errands completely oblivious to the fact that no one could reach her.

But even as he considered the thought, he discarded

it. Something felt wrong. He drove to the station and caught sight of the yellow note tacked to the door. He bounded from the Durango and ripped the note free.

"Need to talk. Meet you at your place."

He returned to the Durango, wasting little time in hitting the highway again. If she'd been at his place, she would've called. She must've returned to her place to pick up Saaski. She'd never leave the dog alone for the night and he knew she'd dropped him off before leaving for Dr. Seryn's place.

Pressing the pedal harder, he picked up speed, unable to outrun the very real feeling that he was racing a clock that was counting down to something terrible.

Chapter 22

"You're going to get caught," Iris said. "It's not like I won't be noticed."

"Of course, I'm counting on it. You see, when Sundance finds your body he'll discover you were attacked by someone he knows and has suspected all along, that will cause him to stop looking up my family tree. You see, he thinks it's my father committing the crimes. Laughable really. My father couldn't do what I do. He doesn't have the balls. He's a bureaucrat through and through."

"Why does Sundance think it's your father?" Iris asked, not really caring, just trying to keep the sociopath from jumping her.

"The ketamine connection," he answered. "He's half-right. My father was my connection to the drug—it was the easiest drug to come by when I started doing this as a teenager and my dad always had it in stock—and I've since become comfortable with it."

"So who are you setting up?" Her gaze swept the kitchen looking for a suitable weapon but nothing aside from the heavy dish in her hand seemed plausible.

"Curious little cat, aren't you?" He grinned. "Okay, I'll bite. Brett Duncan. My poor grant guy. Who knew the paper pusher was a sadist at heart? The evidence is overwhelming, though. You see, I always keep a memento of my girls. And when they find Brett with a suicide note and a pair of your panties in his hand… it'll be sufficient to close the case."

She hid her revulsion, fighting the urge to gag knowing Chad had kept a pair of her panties. "You killed him," she concluded in a tight voice, wishing she had a gun in her hand so she could blow Chad's head off.

He smiled in answer. "I hate loose ends and, besides, he was incredibly annoying and a terrible wingman." His gaze hardened. "As much as I'm enjoying our chat—almost as much as I did our chat at the deli cart. Your pain was so raw, so visceral, I carried the memory with me the rest of the day and into the night—I can't linger any longer. Duty calls." He produced a syringe and advanced toward her. She heaved the deep-dish casserole, hitting him squarely in the chest, and bolted for the door.

He roared with pain but charged after her. She ran through the doorway and slammed into her Bronco, fumbling for the door with clumsy fingers, panic causing her to make mistakes. She got the door open but her head was wrenched back by a fist buried in her long hair. She managed a scream before he cut off her airway, but she stomped his instep and jabbed his midsection with her sharp elbow. He grunted and swore in pain, loosening his grip enough for her to get two fingers into her mouth to whistle loud and shrill.

"We're in the middle of nowhere, sweetheart," he said from between gritted teeth. "Who do you think is going to save you?"

She caught movement in her peripheral vision and screamed, *"Al-tah-je-jay!"*

Saaski, a black blur of motion as if hell had opened up and released a hound, launched himself at Chad with a snarl, clamping down on his arm like a vise with teeth.

Chad screamed and twisted, trying desperately to pry Saaski's jaws from his flesh. Iris heard bone crunch and blood sprayed as teeth punctured an artery.

Iris gasped, her hand going to her throat where Chad had bruised her larynx, but she didn't give Saaski the command to stop. She knew he'd hold Chad there until his arm fell off. If she waited too long, he'd bleed to death.

And would that be so bad?

"Help," Chad screamed, his voice choking on pain and terror. "Oh, God, help me!" Chad tried hitting Saaski with his free hand but it only caused Saaski to clamp down more viciously, and Chad's eyes rolled up into his head as the agony and shock of having his limb nearly torn off almost knocked him out.

She turned as the sound of a vehicle tearing up her driveway drowned out the agonized screams and snarls. Sundance rushed past her to skid to a stop when he saw Saaski mangling Chad into hamburger.

"Call him off, Iris," he demanded, his face white from all the blood splattered in the dirt, his hand going to his holster.

"Why?"

"Because you don't want his blood on your conscience."

She gave him a steady stare. "It wouldn't be." And it was true. She felt no guilt. In fact, she felt nothing.

Sundance's stomach roiled when he saw the mess that'd become Chad's arm. The man had already lost consciousness from the blood loss. He was very nearly dead and he would most certainly die if Iris didn't call off her dog. But one look at Iris and he saw murderous rage coupled with shock, which didn't bode well for anyone.

"Iris," he said sharply to get her attention. It worked and she turned to regard him dispassionately. "Call off Saaski before I have to shoot him."

Her eyes followed his hand as it rested on his gun.

"Don't you dare shoot my dog," she hissed at him, her eyes wild.

He stared her down. "Then call him off. Or I will have to."

Glaring, she gave a Navajo command to Saaski and the dog immediately dropped Chad's arm and trotted over to her. She rubbed his black head, murmuring soft words of praise, and Sundance checked Chad to see if he was still alive. A weak and thready pulse beat beneath his fingers. He spoke into his radio. "I need an ambulance at Iris's place. Immediately."

Iris continued to stroke and praise Saaski, avoiding Chad's mangled body altogether.

"He was going to kill me and frame someone else for it," she said, regarding him with the cold eyes of a stranger. "I won't apologize for defending myself. He was trespassing and he threatened me." She gathered Saaski by the collar and started to walk toward the house, and then she turned to him. "He also killed

Brett Duncan. You might want to inform the man's family."

Sundance watched as Iris disappeared into the house, closing the door firmly behind her, locking out the carnage left behind and him with it.

Iris moved on autopilot, finding Saaski a treat for saving her life and then going straight to her room. The shakes had returned as the full impact of everything that had just happened began to manifest. She'd watched as her dog nearly mangled someone to death and she'd felt no remorse, no regret.

He deserved to die. For every woman he'd destroyed as part of his sick little game; for every young girl from whose life he'd removed all joy; for everything he'd done and more.

She collapsed on her bed, burying her face in the pillows, everything feeling and smelling foreign to her now. She didn't like to think of herself as capable of such dispassionate cruelty but she'd proven herself wrong. She was capable of vicious payback.

She waited for the shame to follow. It didn't.

But then nothing followed. Not shame, not sadness, not horror. She supposed that wasn't normal but she couldn't deal with that right now. Her mind was numb and she welcomed the disassociative feeling as she floated above the situation, removed and apart.

Her eyes drifted shut and she fell into the deepest sleep since the attack.

She could rest because her attacker was in custody and would most likely die before he reached the hospital.

All things considered, it was probably the best outcome.

Too bad Sundance wouldn't see it that way.

* * *

Sundance paced outside the emergency room bay doors. Chad was in there, fighting for his life. He'd lost a lot of blood and the outcome wasn't favorable.

He wanted him to live so he could kill him.

How could he have been so blind? To have the rapist right in plain sight, laughing it up behind his back as he chatted and traded jokes, even shared personal details, burned like hydrochloric acid on bare skin. Worse, he'd thought Chad was his friend. Anything he might've felt for Chad in deference to their years shared together as children, died without a whisper.

His cell phone buzzed and he reluctantly went outside to take the call. It was Russell Jacy.

"I got some news you might want to hear," he said. "We found a match on the fingerprints but you're not going to believe who it matched up to."

Sundance's mouth thinned, knowing the answer. "Chad Brown, Bureau of Indian Affairs liaison," he answered, eliciting a grunt of surprise from Russell.

"How'd you know?"

Sundance rubbed his forehead, easing the ache from gritting his teeth while he waited for news on Chad. "Yeah, I'm in the E.R. right now because Iris's dog nearly killed him when he attacked her."

Russell whistled low. "No kidding?"

"Wish I were. Seems Iris figured out it was him and he was tying up loose ends. He killed and framed another guy for the crimes. We're processing the body now. We searched Chad's home and found a treasure trove of evidence—panties from his victims—I suspect when we compare forensic evidence to a bunch of unsolved rapes in American-Indian country we'll find him at the center. I'm still trying to make sense of everything."

"Damn," Russell said, taking in the information. "I'll relay the information to our investigators to reopen the cold cases. How bad off is the perp?"

"He might not make it."

"Well, maybe that's for the best."

"Yeah, well, I doubt his father is going to feel that way. He's a top dog in the BIA." Sundance swore under his breath as he considered all that was at stake and how many projects Chad had put his touch all over. Likely, they could kiss goodbye all that promised grant money. He needed to get off the phone before his sour mood made him unbearable. "I have to check on the suspect. Keep me in the loop with your investigation so I can add the supplement to the report. Thanks for all your help."

"You got it."

Sundance returned to the emergency room and found Mya looking for him. Her eyes were troubled. "I knew you'd want to know…he's alive but we couldn't save his arm. They're stabilizing him so they can airlift him to a bigger facility with more resources."

Sundance let out an audible breath. As much as he wanted the man to die for his crimes, he also wanted justice for Chad's victims and he was sure there were far more than they knew about. Dead men never gave up their secrets while men facing the death penalty were more apt to cooperate. Chad was going to need to wheel and deal if he wanted to escape lethal injection. Personally, Sundance would rather the man fried but that wasn't going to happen. He tried to keep his mind from going to the places in his memory when they'd been friends. Anytime he found himself slipping into grief over the loss, he reminded himself that the friendship he'd thought he'd shared with Chad had been an illusion. He'd never truly known Chad Brown. And then Sundance ruthlessly severed the tie. What Chad had done to Iris was bad enough but to know he'd raped so many more…it curdled Sundance's stomach. But apparently, blood was thicker than water, because Big Daddy was looking for high-priced lawyers to represent his son, no matter that his son was a monster.

Mya's light touch on his shoulder brought him back to the moment. "Have you talked to Iris yet?"

"She doesn't want to see me," he stated, a lead ball clunking in his gut.

"She was in shock. You two need to talk. You need each other," Mya said. "Especially now that it looks as if Chad is going to be all right and this case will likely go to trial. The prosecution is going to need her testimony. Don't make her go through that alone."

Sundance glared. Did Mya think he wanted her to face this alone? It wasn't his choice. Iris had shut him out when he wouldn't let Saaski eat the man. She blamed him for letting him live. "If she needs me, she knows where to find me."

Mya's mouth pinched and she frowned. "You're both mirrors of one another, stubborn as a mule and just as thickheaded. Remember when you went to her and snapped her out of her funk the first time? You're the only person who can do that for her. You both need to accept the events as they unfolded and move on as a team."

"Mya—"

"I mean it. I've spent the last few years watching you two circle one another, not willing to budge an inch out of stubborn pride and now when you need each other the most you're determined to keep your distance. Well, knock it off and start acting like grown-ups for a change." She drew a breath and added, "I've never seen two people more perfect for one another and that's the truth. Please go to her."

Sundance could sense the logic and reason within Mya's impassioned speech but he was still shocked by the look of murder in Iris's eyes that day. If he hadn't arrived, Chad would be dead and she'd have let it happen. It was his job to uphold the law, not look the other way just because it served someone's thirst for vengeance. He wanted the man dead, too, but that wasn't the way things worked. It wasn't like he could notch an arrow and let it fly like his ancestors would've done. He was torn between two worlds and she, of all people, should recognize that fact.

Chapter 23

Gradually, the numbness of Iris's brain had worn off and she was left with a heartbreaking sadness that permeated her entire being. She went through the motions of living but since Sundance had kept his distance, too busy with the tail end of the case, she'd realized how foolish she'd been to push him away.

Had she really expected Sundance to look the other way while Saaski tore apart another human being? Shame filled her cheeks with heat and a tear slipped from her eyes. But as her gaze alighted on Saaski, her beloved defender, she felt nothing but gratitude. She knew she faced an uphill battle. Chad's father was already calling for Saaski's death, saying the dog was a menace—completely glossing over the fact that Chad had been ready to kill her. Sundance had found the syringe, loaded with enough ketamine to kill a horse, on the gravel where Chad had dropped it when Saaski had attacked. A shudder followed. She'd been seconds from death. She'd do what she had to to protect Saaski, even if it meant draining her savings to hire her own fancy lawyer because there was no way she was putting down her dog.

She wanted to go to Sundance and apologize for putting him in a bad position after everything he'd done for her, but she couldn't find the words to make it right. This was one of those things that ate at you like a flesh-devouring disease. It would sit between them, destroying the love that had sprung and flourished under the most adverse circumstances.

She dropped her face on to her hands, sobbing as reality hit her hard.

Chad Brown had taken so much from her, more than her body, or her dignity…he'd taken her soul mate.

Sundance tried to go about his day—he was damn sure busy enough with all the follow-up that came with the case—but Iris's shadow followed him. Maybe what Mya had said had seeped into his brain but it was becoming more difficult to stay away. He told himself he was just honoring Iris's wishes but that was a bunch of beaver crap and he was man enough to admit it.

He was staying away because he was afraid.

He was afraid of seeing Iris differently, of never being able to wash away the stain of that day from his mind. Of seeing her condemnation for not realizing the true menace had been right in front of him the whole time. That burned. He felt like a fool but worse, he felt like he'd let everyone down.

But after three weeks of dodging Iris at the clinic and pushing away any thought that drew him to her, he was finished with lying to himself. It simply wasn't working. She was a part of him. At night, he reached for her in his sleep, awakening abruptly when he found himself alone in the bed; when he drove past her house, he strained to see if her Bronco was parked outside; he stared at his cell phone hoping she would call.

And frankly, he was over it. Like Mya said, he needed to handle this situation and either make a clean cut or make amends because he couldn't live in this hellish limbo.

It was late and Iris was likely home in bed. He went straight there, not giving himself a chance to change his mind.

But as he pulled into her driveway, his heart contracted painfully when he saw the house dark and her Bronco gone.

Obviously, she'd made plans and they didn't involve him—a fact that he hated. Throwing his Durango into Reverse, he decided to go home. Maybe things would look better in the morning. Hell, maybe he just needed some damn sleep.

But when he finally pulled into his own driveway he was stunned to see Iris's Bronco in the pale moonlight. He bounded to the front door and let himself in. Saaski, asleep by the woodstove, perked up at the sound of someone entering but settled once again when he recognized Sundance's scent.

The house was dark except for a small bedside lamp in his bedroom, that threw off weak light.

He found Iris curled in his bed and tears of relief sprung to his eyes. In that bed was the woman of his dreams and if she'd give him the chance he'd gladly spend the rest of his life showing her the depth of his love and affection. He ground the tears from his eyes and walked toward the bed, feeling as if he'd just been given the keys to the promised land after a long journey.

Iris had fallen asleep waiting for Sundance. She'd made the decision to go to him, to perhaps figure this thing out between them, to see if anything was salvageable but when he hadn't come home, she'd simply drifted off with the soothing comfort of Sundance's scent all around her.

She awoke to find Sundance coming toward her, pulling his shirt off as he went. They held each other's gaze for a long moment, both drinking in the sight of one another.

"I went to your house looking for you," he said, achingly broken.

"I came here looking for you," she whispered. She realized, her heart spasming hard, that the shine in his eyes was from tears and she reached out to him. He didn't hesitate and went straight into her arms. They held each other tightly as she rained soft kisses against his face. "I'm so sorry for what I said. Can you ever forgive me?"

"There's nothing to forgive," he said roughly, pressing her against him, burying his nose in her neck. "It's me who needs your forgiveness. I should've figured out that it was Chad. I should've seen the clues…I put you in danger—"

She shushed him with the urgent press of her mouth against his. "Stop that. You couldn't have known. You did the best you could. Don't take that on. You don't deserve it. I was wrong to expect you to look the other way while Saaski killed the miserable SOB. I'm so sorry for putting you in that position. I wasn't thinking straight and you were right. Watching him die would've stained my soul worse than anything he'd already done to me. Thank you for protecting me from myself during my worst hour. I love you for it and so much more."

He stared into her eyes and she saw love shining back at her. "In your chest beats the heart of a warrior. It's what I love about you. Never change. Your strength is beautiful to me."

"As is yours to me," she said, tears spilling from her eyes as they clutched one another, afraid to let go, hating the time they'd wasted. Her soul cried out to his and finally, lying chest to chest, sharing each other's warmth, she felt an answering joy that washed over the ugliness they'd been through, painting everything in hues of light and happiness.

She was grateful for his intervention because he'd been right in that she wouldn't have wanted Chad's blood on her conscience. Now he would face a trial and she'd gladly testify to send him away to rot.

It was odd to hear the details unfold as more evidence piled up against Chad Brown. In addition to murdering Brett, every reservation he'd worked for under the auspices of the BIA had unsolved rape cases perpetrated by him. The man had cleverly inserted himself within positions of authority, all the while ingratiating himself to the tribes so no one ever suspected him of his crimes. Last she heard, Chad was trying to broker a deal for a more lenient sentence in exchange for previously unknown cases. So far the number of victims was in the high thirties. Privately, Iris drew comfort in the memory of Saaski taking Chad down. For all the pain that man had inflicted on others, losing an arm hardly seemed adequate compensation. But she'd take what she could get.

Iris settled into a contented drowsy state and before she drifted back to sleep, she sighed with happiness.

This was heaven—and she and Sundance had earned their place in it.

Epilogue

Iris sat, tense and holding her breath, gripping Sundance's hand tightly enough to elicit a wince on his part, as the judge returned from her quarters to deliver her judgment on Saaski's fate.

The judge, a woman in her late-sixties and something of a curmudgeon in judicial circles, glanced in the direction of Paul Brown and his high-price attorney and then in the direction of Iris and Sundance with their attorney before saying in a voice that brooked no argument, "In light of the overwhelming evidence, I dismiss this case on the grounds that the dog was on private property and reacting to a significant threat to Ms. Beaudoin." She looked to the bailiff. "See to it that the dog is returned immediately to his owner."

Paul Brown shot up, in spite of his attorney's urging to remain silent and shouted, "That dog nearly killed

my son. He tore his arm off. He's a menace and a threat
to society—"

"The only threat is your son," the judge interrupted
coolly, her eyes flashing. "The dog reacted appropriately.
Case dismissed. Now get out of my courtroom. You've
wasted my time with this case."

Paul Brown's fleshy lip trembled and in the weeks
since Iris had seen him last, he looked like an old man.
Iris felt sorry for him. He'd had no idea he'd raised a
monster. But that was his problem.

She smiled up at Sundance, who shared her relief.
"Shall we go liberate Saaski?" he asked, returning her
smile.

"Yes," she answered joyfully. "I can't wait to see him
again. It hasn't been the same without him."

They drove to the animal shelter where Saaski had
been quarantined, and after Sundance handled the
paperwork, the shelter attendant brought an exuberant
Saaski from the kennels.

Iris teared up and she laughed with joy as her dog
bounded straight to her. She gathered the dog in her
arms, giggling as he laved her face with doggy kisses
and communicated how much he missed her during
his incarceration. She fished in her pocket for a doggie
treat and gleefully gave it to him. "What a good boy,"
she crooned, rising with the leash in her hand.

She caught Sundance's amusement sparkling in his
eyes. "I think I've found my competition," he teased.
"I'm not sure there's ever a way you'll love me as much
as you love Saaski."

Iris laughed openly, hooking her arm through his as
they went to the Durango. She peered up at him with
adoration and love in her heart, knowing she'd never

love anyone the way she loved Sundance. He owned a piece of her soul and that was the plain truth of it.

But it was good to keep a man on his toes.

"We'll see." She gave him a coy smile. "Let's go home."

Home. Together. As it should be.

* * * * *

Mya Jonson's past catches up to her when FBI Agent Angelo Tucker returns to the reservation. Be sure to look for Kimberly Van Meter's next Harlequin Romantic Suspense, COLD CASE REUNION, wherever Harlequin books are sold!

Harlequin

ROMANTIC
SUSPENSE

COMING NEXT MONTH

Available July 26, 2011

#1667 DOUBLE DECEPTION
Code Name: Danger
Merline Lovelace

#1668 SPECIAL OPS BODYGUARD
The Kelley Legacy
Beth Cornelison

#1669 COLD CASE REUNION
Native Country
Kimberly Van Meter

#1670 BEST MAN FOR THE JOB
Meredith Fletcher

You can find more information on upcoming Harlequin® titles, free excerpts and more at
www.HarlequinInsideRomance.com.

HRSCNM0711

REQUEST YOUR FREE BOOKS!
2 FREE NOVELS PLUS 2 FREE GIFTS!

ROMANTIC
S U S P E N S E

Sparked by Danger, Fueled by Passion.

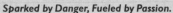

YES! Please send me 2 FREE Harlequin® Romantic Suspense novels and my 2 FREE gifts (gifts are worth about $10). After receiving them, if I don't wish to receive any more books, I can return the shipping statement marked "cancel." If I don't cancel, I will receive 4 brand-new novels every month and be billed just $4.49 per book in the U.S. or $5.24 per book in Canada. That's a saving of at least 14% off the cover price! It's quite a bargain! Shipping and handling is just 50¢ per book in the U.S. and 75¢ per book in Canada.* I understand that accepting the 2 free books and gifts places me under no obligation to buy anything. I can always return a shipment and cancel at any time. Even if I never buy another book, the two free books and gifts are mine to keep forever.

240/340 HDN FEFR

Name _____ (PLEASE PRINT) _____

Address _____ Apt. # _____

City _____ State/Prov. _____ Zip/Postal Code _____

Signature (if under 18, a parent or guardian must sign)

Mail to the **Reader Service:**

IN U.S.A.: P.O. Box 1867, Buffalo, NY 14240-1867
IN CANADA: P.O. Box 609, Fort Erie, Ontario L2A 5X3

Not valid for current subscribers to Harlequin Romantic Suspense books.

Want to try two free books from another line?
Call 1-800-873-8635 or visit www.ReaderService.com.

* Terms and prices subject to change without notice. Prices do not include applicable taxes. Sales tax applicable in N.Y. Canadian residents will be charged applicable taxes. Offer not valid in Quebec. This offer is limited to one order per household. All orders subject to credit approval. Credit or debit balances in a customer's account(s) may be offset by any other outstanding balance owed by or to the customer. Please allow 4 to 6 weeks for delivery. Offer available while quantities last.

Your Privacy—The Reader Service is committed to protecting your privacy. Our Privacy Policy is available online at www.ReaderService.com or upon request from the Reader Service.

We make a portion of our mailing list available to reputable third parties that offer products we believe may interest you. If you prefer that we not exchange your name with third parties, or if you wish to clarify or modify your communication preferences, please visit us at www.ReaderService.com/consumerchoice or write to us at Reader Service Preference Service, P.O. Box 9062, Buffalo, NY 14269. Include your complete name and address.

HRS11B